MW00873579

LIGHT THE FIRE

A HER ELEMENTAL DRAGONS STORY

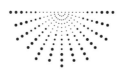

ELIZABETH BRIGGS

Copyright © 2019 by Elizabeth Briggs

LIGHT THE FIRE, A Her Elemental Dragons Story

All rights reserved. This book or any portion thereof may not be reproduced or used in any manner whatsoever without the express written permission of the publisher except for the use of brief quotations in a book review.

This is a work of fiction. Names, characters, businesses, places, events and incidents are either the products of the author's imagination or used in a fictitious manner. Any resemblance to actual persons, living or dead, or actual events is purely coincidental.

Cover art © Lori Follett of Hell Yes Designs

ISBN (paperback) 9781790535491

ISBN (ebook) 9781948456005

www.elizabethbriggs.net

For the ones who came before us to light the way

CHAPTER ONE

The giant brazier flared bright, beckoning me closer. I picked up a scrap of bark and a pointed piece of obsidian from the nearby pile as I considered the flickering flames, along with my future. While a man beside me debated what to write with a frown, I quickly carved my wish on the tiny bit of wood. When I was finished, I read the words once before sending the bark into the fire, where it blackened and curled almost immediately and soon turned to ash and flame. As the Fire God accepted my offering I bowed low and said a small prayer that he'd grant my wish and give me guidance, before I turned back to the celebration. Not that I expected him to answer, of course. But it *was* tradition.

The center of Sparkport was packed tonight with nearly everyone in the village crammed into its town square.

Torches lit up the darkness, adults made wishes at the brazier, and children pranced across the dirt road flying red dragon kites in the air. Fire dancers performed on a stage nearby, their flames leaving trails of light as they twirled in time to the lively music. I moved through the crowd toward one of merchant stalls lining the road, brushing past people in their finest clothes who were dancing together or eating special treats.

The Fire Festival was one of the five celebrations in honor of the Gods and the Dragons, and here in the Fire Realm it was the biggest holiday of the year. My family had been preparing our bakery's stall for weeks, while my sisters and I had spent months sewing our gowns. Mine was a flame red dress with a black lace trim that hugged my body in a way that turned a few heads. An obsidian pendant that belonged to my mother rested between my full breasts, and my blond hair had been tied up with red and black ribbon, though some wispy hairs had already escaped it.

I approached my family's stall with its familiar scent of warm bread and baked sugar. My mother stood inside it, offering one of our signature mini volcano cakes to a child and her father. My older sister Krea was putting out more chocolate-coated flame cookies, while our youngest sister Loka was sneaking one of the fried crab cakes into her mouth. I arched an eyebrow at her and she wiped her mouth with an impish grin.

"Welcome back, Calla," Mom said with a smile. "Did you make a wish?"

“I did. Has it been busy?” I asked, as I stepped behind the stall to join them.

"Very," Mom said. "We're going to run out of those volcano cakes before midnight at this rate."

"All because of Krea’s hard work,” I said.

"Thank you,” my older sister replied, ducking her head so her pale hair partially covered her face. “I had no idea they'd be so popular."

Krea was the one who had come up with the design for the tiny domed chocolate cakes filled with strawberry cream, then topped them with frosting to look like lava. She had true artistic talent, while Loka prided herself on finding the most delicious combinations of food—usually by tasting them herself. Together they would make my mother proud when they took over the bakery. And me? I could bake, certainly, but I didn't have the talent for making pastries beautiful like Krea, and I didn't have the knack for coming up with new recipes like Loka. I'd likely find myself serving customers in the front of the shop my entire life—or I’d be passed off to help my future husband with whatever his trade was.

I wished I had a talent like my sisters, but so far nothing had emerged. I was passably good at many things—sewing, baking, candle making—but an expert in none. Instead I preferred to spend my time reading, but books were in short supply in a small town like Sparkport and scholars were not exactly in demand here either. I had no idea what my future would hold, but now that I was twenty years old I supposed it was time it got started.

As I idly rearranged the boring cheese pastries I'd made —which no one was buying, since they could get them every day in the shop—a loud rumble sounded in the distance from the nearby volcano, Valefire. A moment later the earth trembled under our feet and the crowd murmured and paused until the ground stilled once more. After a few tense seconds, the music started up again and the festival continued on, as if nothing had happened.

"Another earthquake?" I asked, glancing at the tall, flat-topped mountain with its black slopes. Our town was situated in the shadow of Valefire, where the Fire God's temple stood. We'd always respected the volcano, knowing it could awaken at any time, but none of us truly believed it would. Until last month, when the earthquakes had started to increase in frequency and strength.

"It's simply the Fire God showing his approval for the festival," Mom said.

Loka rolled her eyes. "The Fire God hasn't been seen for hundreds of years."

My mother clucked her tongue. "And this is his way of reminding us he's still watching over us, even if we've forgotten him and abandoned his temple. This is why we must celebrate him on holidays like this."

"And pray the volcano stays dormant," I muttered.

"The volcano hasn't erupted in many lifetimes," Mom said, waving our concerns away. "We've always had earthquakes here in Sparkport. There's nothing to be worried about. In fact, you should all go enjoy the festival tonight. I can handle the stall by myself."

"Are you sure?" Krea asked.

"Yes. You'll make me happy by having fun tonight. The Fire Festival is for the young." She shooed Krea and Loka away with a smile. Loka skipped off immediately with a squeal, while Krea hesitated until her betrothed caught her eye and gestured for her to dance with him.

"I'll stay," I said, as Krea slipped away into the crowd.

Mom patted my arm. "That's kind of you, but you should dance too. Derel looks like he could use a break as well."

I followed her gaze to the stall across from ours, run by the local butcher. Mom waved her hand at Sucy, the wife of the butcher and my mother's best friend. Her son, Derel, stood behind the beef kabobs, lemon shrimp, and meatballs they were selling, which I had to admit looked delicious. Behind him, Derel's father tended a large pig roasting on a spit, which would be served at the end of the festival to the entire village. We had a giant volcano cake prepared to go with it, filled with strawberries and cream.

Derel's head turned toward me and he caught me staring at him. I quickly looked away and busied myself in the back of the stall, but the damage was done. It didn't help that Derel was distractingly handsome either, even if I hated to admit it. He had the rich dark skin of his grandparents, who'd moved here from the Earth Realm, with deep brown eyes and gorgeous full lips. Not that I'd spent time much staring at his lips before. Definitely not.

My mother nudged me with her elbow. "Go on, dance with him."

I groaned. "Do I have to?"

"Yes, you do." She clasped her hands together. "I do wish the two of you would get married already. It's all been planned out for you for years!"

"Yes, that's the problem."

"You're lucky. When I was younger I thought I'd never find a husband in this tiny village. If your father hadn't moved to town I'd probably still be alone. I tried to make it easier on you and your sisters by promising you to others as children. Krea and Parin will soon be married. Next it should be you and Derel."

I rolled my eyes. "I doubt Loka will want to marry the man you chose for her."

"Well, I had no idea she'd prefer women or I'd have chosen her a nice wife." She suddenly straightened up. "Oh, here he comes. Be nice." She shuffled away and busied herself at the stall next to ours by offering the chandler some cookies, leaving me to face Derel alone.

As he approached I felt a sense of dread, but also excitement. The Fire Festival made the night feel like anything was possible, even something magical. Like me and Derel getting along for five minutes.

"Care to dance?" he asked in the least convincing voice ever.

I gave him a sickly sweet smile. "With you? Not really."

"Trust me, I'm only here because my mother insisted."

I glanced at my own mother, who gave me a big smile and nodded eagerly. I could practically see visions of dark-skinned grandchildren dancing through her head. "Fine, I'll dance with you. Only because my mother will never stop pestering me until I do."

He took my hand in his strong grip and led me into the square to join the other dancing couples. This dance was an upbeat one, and we switched off clasping hands and spinning and twirling until my heart beat fast and I was almost —*almost*—having a good time with Derel. It didn't hurt that he was an excellent dancer either.

When the music slowed he clasped my hand and pulled me close against his toned body. "Is your mother pressing you to get married like mine is?"

"Always." Though arranged marriages had fallen out of fashion generations ago—much to my mother's dismay—from the time Derel and I were born we'd been promised to each other, whether we liked it or not. And trust me, we did not. The worst part was that if we hadn't been forced together at every opportunity and told how perfect we were for each other, maybe we would have gotten along and fallen in love in our own time. Now we would never know.

"Maybe we should just do it already to get them off our backs," he said, as his hand slowly smoothed down my back.

I let out a sharp laugh to hide how shocked I was at his words, and how much I didn't hate the idea when it came from him. Too bad I knew he wasn't serious. How could he be? We hated each other—always had, always would. "Is that your version of a romantic proposal?"

"I'm going for practical, not romantic. But if romance is what you want..." His smoldering eyes met mine in a way that made my breath catch, especially as he pulled me tighter against him. My gaze dropped to his sensual mouth and I thought, not for the first time, what it would be like to kiss him. As his fingers curled around my chin and he looked at me in the same way, I knew he was thinking about it too.

I shook my head to break the spell he'd cast over me. "Definitely not. I'm never going to marry you."

Was that disappointment flashing across his face before it returned to his normal, disinterested look? Surely not. "Probably for the best. We'd break poor Falon's heart."

"Falon?" I laughed. "Only because you'd spend less time with him if you were married."

He gave me a look dripping with disdain. "If that's what you think then you're more clueless than I thought."

My smile fell. "What is that supposed to mean?"

"Nothing." Derel shook his head.

Was he suggesting Falon had feelings for me? That was certainly news to me. Falon was our best friend, the one thing in common we had besides our parents, but he'd never been anything more—much to my dismay.

"This dress you have on is quite alluring," Derel said. "Are you sure you're not looking for a proposal tonight?"

"Maybe I am, but not from you." None of the men I wanted would propose to me tonight, so it didn't really matter. But I definitely hadn't worn this for Derel, of all people. "What did you mean about Falon?"

He idly touched the lace at my neck. "The quality is quite fine. Let me guess, Krea made it?"

"No, I did." I shoved against his chest, stepping away from him. I knew he was purposefully baiting me to change the subject, but he always knew exactly how to get under my skin and I couldn't help but respond. "Why are you always so impossible?"

His lips quirked up in a wry smile. "You just bring out that side of me, I suppose."

CHAPTER TWO

When the song ended, Derel took my hand and led me over to Falon, who sipped something hot and steamy from a metal cup. Falon was just as handsome as Derel but in an entirely different way. Where Derel was lithe and toned, Falon was broad and muscular. While Derel was dark, Falon was bright. When Derel was rude, Falon was kind.

"It's your turn," Derel said to Falon. "I'm done dancing with her."

"And so gracious about it," I muttered.

"Don't pretend you didn't enjoy it." He gave me one last smoldering look before stalking back to his parents' stall.

"Shall we dance?" Falen asked with a smile, offering me his hand.

My nerves instantly calmed as I entwined my fingers with his. "I'd like that."

Falon led me back into the square amid the other revelers. He rested his hand on my waist, but kept his distance from me. I tried not to hide my disappointment, especially after Derel had sparked the idea in my head that Falon might have feelings for me. But that was ridiculous. Falon and I had been friends ever since his family had moved to our village when he was five, but there had never been anything more between us. Unfortunately.

Falon's family worked as carpenters, and his strong, rough fingers felt good against my own. He was a large man, the kind who'd gained his muscles working long hours, and I wished he would pull me against his chest like Derel had done. I'd secretly harbored feelings for Falon for years, but he'd never shown even a hint that he saw me as anything more than a friend. If only he would give me a sign he wanted more, maybe we could ease the awkwardness between us. But he never did.

"You look beautiful tonight," he said, making my heart skip a beat. "That dress is lovely."

"Thank you. Krea designed it for me, although I all the sewing," I admitted. Unlike Derel, Falon didn't judge me or tease me. I could tell him anything.

"No doubt the Fire God will smile upon your efforts. Did you throw a wish in the brazier?"

"Of course. Did you?"

He nodded. "What did you wish for?"

I gave him a teasing smile as I played with the collar of his shirt. "You know we're not supposed to tell."

"Oh, come on. We're best friends. Surely you can tell me what you wished for."

There it was. Best friends. That was how he saw me, and that would never change. "Definitely not."

His blue eyes danced with amusement. "Let me guess. You wished for love."

"Love?" I said, with a short laugh.

"That's what everyone wishes for."

"Not me. I asked the Fire God to show me what my path should be. To give me a hint about my role in this town and what I should do with my life." I tilted my head. "What about you? Did you wish for love?"

"No, of course not," he said a little too quickly, before looking away. "I wished for the same thing as you, pretty much. To have a good future."

"Uh huh." I smiled at him. "Who's the lucky lady you have your eye on?"

"There's no one." He fingers tightened around my waist. "You're the only lady I ever spend time with, after all."

That was true. But if he'd wished for love and I was the one he wanted to be with, why didn't he just tell me so? Was he worried about Derel? He must know I could barely stand to be in Derel's presence, even if my body was physically attracted to him at times. Or was Falon concerned we'd ruin our friendship? Or that I didn't feel the same for him?

Maybe he needed a little hint as to my feelings. I pressed my lips to his cheek as the song ended. "It's okay if you did wish for love, you know."

He turned his head toward me, so that my mouth nearly touched his own. I felt both of us breathing heavily, locked in a close embrace that had somehow shifted from friendly to more. I slid my fingers up into his short blond hair while he looked at me in a new way and opened his mouth. Hope rose up in my chest that he might finally confess his feelings, but then a hand landed on my shoulder and ruined the moment.

"My turn," a low voice said.

I looked up at Blane in surprise as he swept me into his arms in a lover's embrace, so different from the way Falon had been holding me and even more intimate than the way Derel had danced with me. I should have pushed him away or told him to stop, but instead I found my traitorous arms sliding around his neck and my heart racing as we began to dance. I glanced back at Falon, who gave me a friendly smile and a nod, before the crowd swallowed us up.

"When did they let you out of jail?" I asked Blane, mainly to distract myself from the way he felt. And smelled. And looked. Everything about Blane was irresistible, from the sexy drawl of his voice, to his dark tousled hair, to his tall, muscular body. And trust me, I'd tried to resist.

"Jail" was really the basement of the chandler's house, since Sparkport was too small to have an actual prison and Blane was the only person who was ever thrown into it on a regular basis. Usually by Derel and Falon, who acted as the town guard on most nights.

"This morning," Blane said, with a roguish grin. "Falon

took pity on me. He didn't want me to miss the Fire Festival, after all."

"What was it this time?"

He lifted one shoulder in a casual shrug. "I appropriated some wine from that grumpy old merchant Carik. He had plenty, trust me."

I sighed. Carik was known to cheat people out of their money, but that didn't excuse Blane's theft. "I shouldn't even be dancing with you."

"Why not? Embarrassed to be seen in my arms?"

"Something like that."

"Too bad you like it so much." His lips brushed against my neck and sent shivers down my spine. The worst part was, he was right. Blane was the village bad boy, always getting into trouble, but for some reason I couldn't resist him even though I knew it was wrong. My family would never let me be with him, and Blane wasn't the type who'd want to get married anyway. But I couldn't stay away.

Blane was the one of the two men I'd kissed in my life, and I knew he wanted more from me too, but I'd held myself back so far. It was difficult though because the man practically oozed sexuality. Just being around him made me damp between my legs. And his touch? It made me crave more every time.

“You wore this dress for me, didn't you?” he asked, his lips trailing down to the spot next to my pendant, dangerously close to my breasts. I gasped, worried about people watching us, though I was finding it hard to care at the moment.

“Don’t be silly,” I said, though my breathless voice gave me away.

“You look so very tempting in it. The only way you’d look better is with it pooled at your feet.” His hand ran down my back to rest on my bottom possessively. "Will you meet me later tonight?"

"I can't."

"That's too bad." He took my earlobe between his teeth and I let out a gasp. "I can't stop thinking about you."

"Well, you should. Stop, I mean." Gods, Blane made me flustered in a way no one else did. "We both know we don't have a future together. My mother is pushing for me to marry soon, after all, and—”

He pulled back, his eyebrows darting up. "Why don't we have a future? Because I'm not good enough for you?"

"No! I just.... I mean... I didn't think you were the kind to settle down.”

"I might surprise you. I could be convinced to settle down...with the right woman." He gave me a look that made me melt, and I thought for sure he would kiss me right there in front of everyone, and I imagined all the things my mother would say afterward and how we'd be gossiped about for weeks or even months, and I decided at that moment I didn't care one bit because it would be worth it for another kiss from Blane. But then he released me. "I've got something to do, but I'll find you later. I promise."

I nodded and swallowed, unable to speak. As he left, I told myself it was for the best that he’d walked away. I could never truly be with Blane, and I didn’t believe he really wanted a serious relationship. Best to put him out of my mind entirely from now on.

But who was I kidding? I'd be counting down the minutes until he returned.

CHAPTER THREE

I looked for Falon again, but he was dancing with one of his sister's friends, and then my eyes caught sight of a dark man standing in the corner with his arms crossed. My mouth fell open at the sight. Roth was here! I didn't think he would come. How long had he been standing there? Had he seen me dance with the others? Was he jealous? Or did he no longer care?

I approached Roth in the shadows with a tentative smile. From this angle I could only see one side of his face, which was devastatingly handsome, as if he'd been sculpted by the Gods themselves. High cheekbones. A perfect masculine nose. A strong jaw. And the rich, auburn hair that was so highly prized in the Fire Realm, which I desperately wanted to run my hands through again.

But when he turned toward me the rest of him became visible under the torchlight, revealing a horrible burn scar that ran down the other side of his face. I knew it bothered him, but to me it only highlighted how beautiful he was. If anything, the imperfection only made him look better to me. Especially since I'd been there when he'd gotten it.

"Calla," he said in a tone that made it clear he wasn't happy to see me. "Why aren't you dancing?"

"I was hoping you'd dance with me."

"You know I don't dance."

"You used to."

"I did." He look away with a scowl. "Before."

Roth had always been rather serious and quiet, but after the accident he'd turned downright brooding. Now I barely ever saw him, and when I did, he tried to push me away. The only times I ever spoke with him was when I found him working on the docks or on the rare occasions he brought crab to the bakery. I was tired of him avoiding me.

I gave him a hesitant smile. "Everyone is dancing. No one will stare, I promise."

"No."

I sighed. "All right. Then why don't we get something to eat? It's been ages since we talked." My voice dropped into nearly a whisper. "I miss you, Roth."

He ran a hand over his face, hiding his scars, a sure sign he was dismayed. "You're very kind, Calla, but I shouldn't have come tonight. I think I'll just go."

"No, please." I took his hand and sparks danced under my skin. Once I'd thought Roth and I might marry. We'd always been close, and two years ago it had flared into more.

He'd confessed his love for me at that Fire Festival, and then invited me out onto his family's boat the next night.

When we were out at sea, we made love for the first time, and I'd never felt so happy before. I was certain he was going to ask for my hand, but then we were attacked by a water elemental. Here, in the Fire Realm, of all places.

The elemental covered my face with water and nearly drowned me, but Roth stepped in to defend me with a torch he'd lit. He managed to save my life and defeat the elemental, but the boat was set on fire in the process. While trying to put out the flames the left side of his body was badly burned, including his face. We were forced to abandon the boat, and I was so weak from nearly drowning he had to pull me back to shore, where he then passed out from the pain.

After that, he hid himself from the world—and from me.

I took a step closer to Roth. "I wish we could be friends again, at least. You know I don't blame you for what happened. If anything, I see you as a hero. You saved us both and—"

"I nearly got you killed and I destroyed my family's boat at the same time." He gestured at his face. "Not to mention, I got a nice reminder of my failure, which I have to see every time I look in a mirror." He turned to leave, but said over his shoulder, "Trust me, Calla. You're better off without me in your life. And now I must go."

"No one's leaving yet," Blane said, with a devious grin. Falon and Derel stood behind him, watching Roth with interest. "Not until I show you something."

Roth cast him a skeptical look. "What is it?"

"Come with me and you'll see. I promise it's worth your time."

Derel snorted. "Last time you said that we got so drunk we spent the next day vomiting."

Blane offered me his hand. "Fine, I'll take Calla by myself. We can have a romantic moment together while you three stay here with the crowd."

"Where are we going?" I asked, intrigued despite myself. Blane was always getting us into trouble, but we all secretly liked it. There wasn't much to do in a small village like this, but Blane always managed to keep things interesting.

"To the beach."

Falon sighed. "Well, now we have to go to make sure Blane doesn't get Calla in trouble."

"True," Derel said. "Or we could arrest him now and save ourselves the trouble."

Blane rolled his eyes. "You already arrested me once this week. And you let me off, too."

"I'm starting to regret that decision," Fallon said.

Together we all walked over to the docks at the end of town, where I saw Loka dart off with another girl, both of them holding hands and giggling. I smiled, hoping she'd find some happiness tonight.

Blane carried a torch and led us to the beach, where the dark waves were slowly lapping at the shore. I held up my skirt as we stepped into the sand, but then arms swept me off my feet from behind. I found myself in Falon's strong arms and let out a gasp.

"Didn't want you to ruin that pretty gown you'd worked so hard on," he said with a smile.

"Thank you." First the dance, and now this. I wasn't sure Falon had touched me so much in my life before this night. Not that I was complaining.

Blane kept walking through the sand until he reached a cluster of rocks, well away from the lights, sounds, and smells of the festival. He bent down to remove a hidden sack and opened it up to reveal a dozen long tubes with pointed ends. Fireworks.

"Where did you get these?" I asked.

"In Flamedale on my last trip." Blane was the only one of us who had ever left the village. His mother died in childbirth, and his father died ten years later after years of being an alcoholic. After that Blane took whatever jobs he could get in order to keep food in his stomach and a roof over his head. He was the best fighter in the village and often worked as a mercenary for traveling merchants or whatever else was required of him. Rumor had it he had joined up with some bandits at one point too. But he always came back to Sparkport.

"Did you steal these?" Falon asked, as he picked up one of the fireworks.

"It doesn't matter how I got them," Blane said.

Derel crossed his arms. "Do you even know how to use them?"

Blane shrugged. "You light this end with fire and aim it at the sky. How hard can it be?"

"You're going to get us all killed," Roth muttered.

"Then Calla had better kiss us first, just in case," Blane said.

My jaw fell open. "All of you?"

Blane grinned. "Why not?"

I was speechless as I glanced between them, though I couldn't help but imagine it. I knew how good it felt to kiss Blane and Roth, and I'd just been in Derel and Falon's arms while we'd danced. I pictured moving from one man to the other, or all of them surrounding me, their hands and mouths sliding across my skin...

The five of us had once been best friends and practically inseparable. When you grew up in a small village it was natural to form close bonds with the other people your age, and for me it was the four of them. But when we got older my feelings for each of them shifted and grew into more. We began spending less time together, especially as we all became busy learning our trades, though I wondered if there was more to it than that. Sometimes I wondered if it was because of me.

I had the opposite of the problem my mother had when she was younger: I had four men I could see potentially marrying, but my relationship with each one was complicated and in the end I was with none of them. Besides, how could I ever pick one when I had feelings for all of them? Yes, even Derel, though I hated to admit it to myself.

I'd heard that in the Air and Water Realms many people took multiple partners the way the Spirit Goddess and the Black Dragon did. Some considered it a way to honor them and believed it was normal to love more than one person.

But here in the Fire Realm we were more traditional and it was almost unheard of—I certainly knew my mother would never approve.

"Now you've scared her," Falon said, snapping me out of my thoughts.

Blane picked up one of the fireworks. "Come on, the town will love it. Help me light one."

"I want no part of this," Roth said, stepping back.

"Nothing is going to happen, I promise. Besides, there's nothing here but sand and water."

"And us," Roth muttered. He threw an arm in front of me, as if to block me from the fireworks.

"Let's do one and see how it goes," Derel said. He was always the first one to jump on Blane's wild plans, despite being the town guard. After he joined in, Falon always did too, and then Roth would finally cave in. And me? I was always happy to be near them, no matter what trouble we were getting into.

I watched as the guys debated the best way to light the fireworks. Eventually they decided to prop one of them up in the sand right next to the water, in case it went wrong.

But then a huge rumble sounded in the distance coming from Valefire. The ground beneath us shook violently, making me lose my footing in the black sand. I clutched onto Roth for support as the world trembled and the mountain roared. We all stared as ominous white smoke burst from its peak in a huge plume, illuminated by an eerie light coming from inside of Valefire.

The volcano had awakened.

CHAPTER FOUR

Blane scooped up his fireworks while the rest of us rushed across the sand back toward Sparkport. Another earthquake swept through the land, this one so strong it made me stumble into Derel, who caught my arm to steady me. Fear made me scramble back up again, along with worry for my family. That rumble had been so loud and there was so much smoke rising into the sky, it made me nervous the volcano could erupt at any moment.

As we entered the village the crowd was screaming and running about, the mood changed from festive to chaotic. The music had stopped, the stage where the dancers had been was on fire, and worst of all, a crack had formed down the middle of the town square. Not large enough to truly injure anyone, but not a good sign either.

Derel kept his arm around me as people shoved and pushed against us in their frenzy, but we lost the other men in the crowd. He didn't let go until we found our family's stalls, where my mother threw her arms around me.

"Calla! I was so worried."

"I'm okay." I gave her a squeeze, and then hugged Krea next.

"Thank you, Derel," Mom said. Now she'd never let up on us getting married. He gave us both a nod, before moving to speak with his own parents at their stall. Mom turned back to me. "Have you seen Loka?"

"She's not here?" I glanced quickly through the crowd, but then remembered seeing her at the docks with that girl. "I think I know where she is. I'll get her quickly."

Mom grasped my hands tightly. "Please be careful, and head back to the house as soon as you find her."

"I will."

I slipped back through the crowd, which was quickly dispersing as people ran to their homes or found shelter in case the volcano began raining lava, rocks, or ash from the sky. We'd all heard tales of when the Fire God was displeased with his subjects and had nearly destroyed the entire Realm with his wrath, and how it wasn't just the lava that had taken so many lives but the poisonous smoke and the fiery rocks that descended on the land. We were close enough to the volcano that if it did erupt and the lava flowed in our direction we could lose all our homes—and possibly our lives.

Long ago, the five Gods had created this world, and each one represented the elements of earth, air, fire, water, and spirit. The Spirit Goddess was their leader, and took the other four Gods as her mates. Later they created the five Dragons to act as their representatives in the world, and then the Gods vanished. Now the five Dragons—Black, Crimson, Azure, Jade, and Golden—ruled over the different Realms and its people, but many people believed the Gods would one day return. I'd never thought it would happen in my lifetime, but now I was starting to change my mind.

I ran back toward the dock, but when I arrived I didn't see a single soul, only the fishing boats tied to the wooden pier. "Loka?" I called out. "Are you here?"

When I couldn't find her I headed down the beach in the opposite direction from where Blane had hidden the fireworks, hoping Loka and her girlfriend might be scared and hiding somewhere. I continued around the bend, calling her name, climbing onto the large rocks where she'd liked to play where we were kids. But I didn't see her anywhere.

She must have gone back to the town. I probably just missed her. Or so I hoped.

As I turned around to head back to Sparkport, I felt a blast of heat and smoke. I blinked it away and came face to face with a giant made of fire, who'd suddenly materialized in front of me.

I screamed and scrambled back, slipping on the wet rocks and falling on my behind with a sharp jolt. I couldn't get away fast enough, my fear causing me to stumble over the rocks and back onto the sand in a mad dash to escape the fiery thing in front of me.

At first I thought it was an elemental, but the one Roth and I had encountered looked like an upside-down teardrop made of swirling water, with arms and glowing eyes. But this was different—it clearly was male, at least in shape, but made entirely of flame and as tall as a house.

And it was coming right for me.

"Calla of the Fire Realm," a voice bellowed out of his burning mouth. He took another step toward me, his flaming feet turning the black sand to glass. "Are you willing to serve your God?"

I froze, panic making my throat clench up, as it slowly dawned on me who was standing before me. The Fire God.

Could it really be him? No one had seen or heard from the Gods in centuries. They were myths and legends, the Fire Temple had been abandoned years ago, and even though I prayed to the Fire God like a good daughter, I could hardly believe he was standing in front of me.

As the shock wore off I considered running and screaming for help, but then he let out a roar. A circle of fire burst up around us, blocking out the rest of the world. Heat coated my skin and terror consumed me, along with sheer awe. Was he going to strike me down?

The blazing eyes seemed to look deep into my soul as he spoke. "You asked for clarity. You wanted a path. You prayed for my guidance. Do you refuse it now?"

Somehow he knew what I'd written and thrown in the brazier. It truly was him. I dropped to my knees, my gown pressing into the sand, and bowed my head at the Fire God. As the terror faded away, I finally found my voice. "What must I do?"

"You will come to the Fire Temple and serve me as High

Priestess. Bring four men to serve as your priests and your mates. Once you arrive, I will give you further instructions. Do you accept my offer?"

"I..." My voice trailed off as his words sunk in. I'd asked for a sign as to what my place in the world would be, but I'd never expected *this*. He was asking me to give up my entire life and walk away from everything I knew to live in the Fire Temple on top of the volcano and serve as his priestess. It was impossible to consider, but he was a God—could I even refuse? Would he strike me down if I did?

And why me? My mother was much more devout than I was. There were many days when I hadn't believed the Gods existed at all, or if I did, I'd cursed them. I had no idea what being his High Priestess even meant. Not to mention, he wanted me to bring four men with me and take them as my mates. I certainly knew the four I'd want, but I couldn't ask them to give up their entire lives for me.

Yet as the shock wore off, a sense of purpose and wonder filled me, like nothing I'd ever known before. I would serve one of the Gods—there was no higher calling than that, especially if they were awakening after all this time. But how would I ever convince the others to go with me? Derel would never leave behind his family's business, Blane was definitely not priest material, and Roth could barely spend a moment alone with me anymore. The only one who might do it out of loyalty was Falon, but I had a hard time seeing him going anywhere without Derel.

"Why four men?" I managed to ask.

"The Spirit Goddess has four mates. The Black Dragon has four mates. My High Priestess must also have four."

I supposed that made sense and, if I was honest, the idea of being with all four men excited me, assuming they would ever agree to it. But they would never consider leaving as long as Sparkport was in danger, and neither would I. "What of the volcano? I can't leave my family behind if there is a risk of it erupting—and I wouldn't be able to reach the Fire Temple if it does."

"Once you arrive at the temple the volcano will become calm again."

I glanced back in the direction of the village, though the rocks blocked it from view, and then sighed. This was my destiny, like it or not. "Yes, I will become your High Priestess."

"Then rise."

I pushed myself up on shaking knees and faced the God in front of me. He moved close, singeing my dress and my hair, and my skin felt like it was going to peel off me. Before I could pull away he reached for me, and then all I knew was fire and heat. It raced along my skin, tore at my flesh, and melted my bones. I was taken apart and reformed. I died and was born again. I was ash and flame, smoke and lava, sparks and coal, and then I was whole again.

As the fire faded away and vanished, I stumbled back—but the Fire God was gone.

CHAPTER FIVE

Somehow I found my way back through the empty town, past the abandoned stalls, discarded dragon kites, and the new crack in the road. I felt so odd, like I was watching myself from a distance, unable to comprehend what had just happened. The Fire God had done something to me—but what?

I was in shock, still in disbelief that I'd said yes to his offer, and now I had a journey ahead of me that I was both excited and nervous about. But first I had to talk to the four men in my life, along with my family. How was I going to explain what had happened on the beach? Would anyone even believe me? I certainly wouldn't.

When I made it back to our home, the door flew open and Loka dashed out. "There you are!" she said as she wrapped her arms around me. "Gods, your dress! What did you do to it?"

I glanced down at myself and saw my crimson gown, which I'd worked so hard on for months, had been torn, covered in sand, and singed in numerous places. I could only shake my head as she led me inside, where the rest of our family waited.

"Thank the Gods you're safe," Mom said, as she swept me into her embrace.

"I'm just glad Loka made it back," I managed to say.

"Yes, she arrived not long after you left to find her. You must have just missed each other." She wiped soot off my face. "Goodness, you look like you had a fight with a hearth and lost. Is the ash from the volcano truly that bad already?"

"No, I..." I sank down into a chair, still shaken. "I have to tell you something."

They sat at the wooden dining table and listened intently while I went over everything that had happened at the beach, which sounded even more unbelievable when I said it all out loud. When I was finished, my sisters glanced at each other skeptically.

"Are you sure you weren't dreaming?" Krea asked.

"Yes, maybe you slipped and hit your head on the rocks," Loka added. "Are you feeling all right?"

I shook my head. "I know it sounds impossible, but it was real. I wish there was a way to prove it to you."

My mother had remained silent the entire time, her mouth frozen in a permanent tight line. But now she said, "There is a way."

"How?" I asked.

"The High Priestess can summon her God's element."

She reached for a candle and set it on the table in front of me. "Try it."

Now I was the one giving skeptical looks. "How do you know?"

A faint smile touched her lips. "My grandmother was also High Priestess, as was her mother, and her mother before that. They could control fire too."

"It's hereditary?" I asked.

"It was, at least in the old days."

"You never told us any of this," Loka said, her eyes huge.

"What happened?" Krea asked. "The Fire Temple has been abandoned for years."

"My grandmother Ara left the temple and married a man here in Sparkport. I don't know why exactly, but my mother believed perhaps Ara grew tired of serving an absent God that no one believed in anymore. Maybe all of the world did stop believing, but now the Fire God is stirring, which means something is changing. And he's chosen you to be part of it. You can't refuse."

"But I don't have any magic," I said.

"Maybe you do now. You said the flames covered you, but you appear unharmed." She rested her hand over mine and gave it a squeeze. "Have faith. He came to you for a reason."

"I'll try," I said, but I didn't have any confidence it would work. My body felt no different than it had before meeting the Fire God. It was my mind that had been shaken.

I reached for the candle and thought of fire, but nothing happened, although I sensed...something. I closed my eyes and remembered how it had felt when the Fire God had touched me and infused me with flames, how they'd become part of my body. Maybe I could channel that out of me now.

The candle wick suddenly burst into a huge flame, so large it made me gasp. My sisters stared at me like they'd never met me before, while my mother had never looked more proud.

She clasped her hands to her chest. "I knew it. Praise the Fire God."

"It's true," Loka whispered. "You really are the High Priestess."

I waved my hand at the fire, and to my surprise, it went out. "Not yet. I still need to travel to the temple. Only then will the Fire God tell me my purpose—and stop the volcano." I swallowed. "And I need to bring four men with me to be my priests."

"Lucky you," Krea said, with a knowing smile.

"That shouldn't be a problem," Mom said. "I'm sure Derel will agree, and those other friends of his probably will too. They all seem to be smitten with you."

"For some strange reason," Loka added as she nudged me with her elbow, making me smile.

"This is such a large thing to ask of them though. They'd be giving up their lives here for one at the temple, and they'd have to all agree to be with me." I glanced at my mother. "Are you sure you're all right with that?"

"As I said, our family is descended from the High Priestesses of the past. My grandmother had four fathers. It's not common in the Fire Realm, but if the Gods demand four husbands for their High Priestess, who are we to argue with them?"

I nodded and ran my hand along the table, feeling the ridges and grooves that I'd known my entire life. "If I do this, I'll be leaving Sparkport forever."

"You can still come visit, I'm sure," Krea said. "The Fire God won't demand you stay in the temple every single moment of your life."

Loka squeezed my hand with a smile. "We can come visit you too. We'll make sure you have enough supplies. It's not far, after all."

I nodded. As she said, Valefire wasn't far—only about a two day walk or so—but the journey up the volcano wouldn't be easy, especially when it was active. I'd have to trust that the Fire God was not sending me to my death and that he would protect me and my men.

Emotion made my throat tight as I glanced between my sisters and my mother. "I'm going to miss you all so much though. And the bakery—will you be okay without me?"

"Of course we will." Mom wiped at her eyes and then gathered me in a hug. "We'll miss you too, but this is your calling. I'm so proud of you, dear."

I hugged my mother back, my eyes filling with tears. I'd wanted guidance, but I hadn't expected my entire life to change this night—or that I'd have to say goodbye to the people I loved.

"We'll take care of Mom," Krea said, as she and Loka hugged me next.

"Don't worry about us. When are you leaving?" Loka asked.

Another small quake rippled under our feet, reminding us of my duty. "Tomorrow. Assuming I can convince the four men to come with me."

Mom jumped to her feet. "I'll start preparing some food for you to take."

"I'll help you pack," Krea said.

I rose in a daze to begin preparations, but then a knock sounded on the door. Mom rushed over to answer it and smiled when she saw it was Derel. "What a lovely surprise."

"Mother wanted me to check on all of you." His dark eyes found me behind the rest of my family, almost like he was seeking me out, but then he turned back to my mother. "Are you well?"

"Yes, thank you. But Calla has something she must speak to you about."

"Is that so?" Derel asked, raising an eyebrow.

I took Derel's arm, leading him outside, away from my nosy family. I closed the door behind me and spoke in hushed tones. "Can you get the others and meet me on the beach in a few minutes? It's important."

His face changed from intrigued to worried. "Is something wrong?"

"No, but I need to ask all of you something. Tonight."

He nodded. "I'll get them."

CHAPTER SIX

I sat on the rock where Blane had hid the fireworks earlier and adjusted my ruined dress, wishing I'd spared a moment to change into a new one. I'd been too busy packing my things and debating how to explain all of this to the four men I hoped would come with me to the temple. If I couldn't convince them, what then?

The volcano had calmed now, perhaps because I'd accepted the Fire God's offer and was doing what he wanted. The four men stood in front of me on the sand, the moonlight illuminating their handsome features. I'd agonized for so long over which man I would marry and how I would ever choose, but now I wouldn't have to—assuming they said yes.

"Is everything all right?" Falon asked.

"When I said we should meet later, I didn't mean with these other guys," Blane muttered.

Roth crossed his arms, looking surly. “Why have you brought us out here in the middle of the night?”

I drew in a deep breath. "There’s something I need to tell you. And more importantly, something I need to ask you. All of you.”

“What is it?” Derel asked.

There was no easy way to say this, so I got right to it. “After the volcano awakened I went looking for my sister on the beach to the north. There I met the Fire God.”

Falon’s brow furrowed. “I don’t understand.”

“What do you mean, you met the Fire God?” Blane asked.

“He came to me looking like a giant flaming man. He said he’s chosen me to be his High Priestess and that I need to go to the Fire Temple to serve him.” I glanced at the volcano, which still had a plume of smoke rising from it. “Only then will Valefire return to sleep.”

The four men gave each other confused and skeptical looks, probably wondering if they should be worried for my sanity or if I was trying to play some kind of prank on them, like we did when we were kids. I sighed and held out my hand, hoping the magic would come to me again this time. A spark flashed and then flickered into a small flame dancing in my palm. Oddly enough, it didn’t burn me at all.

“I know this is hard to believe,” I said, as they all gasped and stared at the fire. “But it’s the truth. I’m leaving tomorrow for the Fire Temple, and I’m here to ask if you will go with me and become my priests.” I swallowed and lowered my eyes. “And my mates.”

Blane raised an eyebrow. "Your *mates*?"

"You want us to become priests?" Falon asked, looking more baffled than ever. "And...share you?"

"How would that even work?" Derel asked.

"And how did you summon fire?" Roth added.

"I don't know," I admitted. "I'm still figuring all of this out myself."

"Did he tell you anything else?" Falon asked.

"No, but he said we would learn more once we arrived at the temple. All I know is that the Fire God chose me and he told me to bring four men with me." I closed my palm over the fire, snuffing it out. "I know this is a lot to ask of you, but I can't imagine choosing any other men as my mates."

"And if we say no?" Roth asked.

"I...suppose I'll have to find others. The Fire God demanded four." I shuddered at the thought of taking strangers as my mates.

Roth ran a hand over his scarred face. "Are you sure you truly want each of us?"

The hint of vulnerability in his voice made my chest ache. "Yes, I am." I met their eyes in turn as I spoke slowly, hesitant to admit the feelings I'd kept inside so long. "I care about all of you so much. For years I've wondered if one of you might become my husband, but I wasn't sure I could ever choose between you. Now I don't have to choose, as long as you all say yes."

None of the four men jumped on my offer, but each one seemed as though they were considering it. I didn't blame them—it was a huge decision that would impact the rest of our lives. Yet with each passing minute, my path became clearer and I began to accept that this was my true calling. I only hoped they agreed to be part of my destiny.

I rose to my feet. "Think on it tonight. I plan to leave at dawn."

"So soon?" Derel asked.

"The sooner I get to the temple the sooner the town will be safe from the volcano."

"What of your family?" Falon asked.

"I'm going to miss them terribly, but this is something I have to do. My mother agreed—she said our family is descended from the last High Priestess. Besides, we'll be able to visit now and then, and our families can come to the temple anytime too. I'll still see my family when I can."

Blane ran a hand through his dark hair. "This is a lot to take in."

"I know, and I'm so sorry. If you're outside my house in the morning, then I'll be honored to have you at my side on this journey. If you decide to stay, I completely understand and won't hold it against you." I gave them all a weak smile. "We'll always remain friends, no matter what you choose."

I stepped off the rocks and began the trek back toward my house to finish packing and try to get some sleep before my long walk to the volcano, though I knew sleep would elude me tonight. I'd be too worried over what the men would decide and what would face me in the days to come.

As I passed the men, Blane's hand shot out and caught my arm. "Wait." He pulled me back toward him, taking me in his arms so suddenly I lost my breath. "I'm going with you."

His mouth descended on mine and he stole a demanding, possessive kiss right in front of the other men. As always, my body melted at his touch and begged for more, even if I worried what the others would think.

When I managed to pull back, I asked, "You are?"

He ran his rough thumb along my sensitive lips. "I don't have anything tying me down here except you. If you leave, I'm going with you."

"I'm going too," Derel said, surprising me even more than Blane.

I spun around to face him. "What about your family? Everyone expects you to take over as the town butcher one day."

He shrugged. "They'll have to find someone else. Besides, my mother would never let me hear the end of it if I didn't go with you."

"Thank you," I said, sliding my arms around him. After a moment's hesitation, he embraced me back, his smoldering eyes staring down at me as if he wanted to kiss me. His hands skimmed down my back, getting distractingly close to my behind. Other than the dance earlier, it was the most intimate we'd ever been together. Most of the time we hated each other...but maybe we didn't. Not really.

"I'm in too," Falon said. "The temple is probably falling apart anyway. You'll need a good carpenter."

I moved into Falon's open arms with a smile. "Yes, we will."

His hug was friendly, though he held me tight against him. I found myself pressing my face to his neck, breathing him in, wishing I was bold enough to press my lips there. Would he kiss me back if I pulled him down to my mouth? Was he going with me because he cared for me too—or only as my friend?

I turned to Roth, the only one who hadn't spoken up, hoping he'd say he was coming too. It had to be the four of them, my closest friends, the men I'd always loved, but he shook his head. "I'm sorry, Calla. Like I said, you're better off without me."

He walked away as sadness dragged me down. I bowed my head, unable to watch him leave, knowing it meant the end for the two of us. For the past few years I'd held on to the hope that he would come around and we'd have a chance at happiness again, but now I knew that had been futile.

"Roth!" Blane called out, as Roth's form vanished in the darkness.

"Let him go," Derel said.

"Are you okay, Calla?" Falon asked, running his hands along my bare arms as if to warm them.

I forced a smile and blinked back tears. "Yes, I'm all right. I didn't really expect any of you to say yes. Especially so quickly. Thank you so much for going on this journey with me and everything that entails." I glanced between the three of them, thinking how lucky I was that they'd agreed to come with me. "Now we should get some rest—we leave at first light."

CHAPTER SEVEN

When I stepped out of my house, I was shocked to see a crowd already waiting for me. I'd always known gossip traveled quickly in a small town like Sparkport, but I had no idea just how fast until now.

"Oh my," Mom said, as she moved out from behind me and took in the throng of people before us. "It seems the entire town's come to see you off."

"How many people did you tell about this?"

She shrugged. "Only Sucy, of course."

I groaned. I should have known. Derel's mother was the town gossip. Then again, he would have to tell her why he was suddenly leaving town, so I supposed it was inevitable that all of Sparkport would soon know about the Fire God's visit and my destiny. Along with my upcoming relationship with four men.

I caught sight of Derel standing with his parents, who

were giving him hugs and wiping at their eyes. Nearby, Falon was saying goodbye to his family too. I felt horrible for taking them away from the people they loved, who'd depended on them to take over their trades in a few years. Falon's brother could take over his family's carpentry business, but Derel's family would have to find themselves a new apprentice butcher now.

Blane, on the other hand, was alone. He leaned against the side of my house with his bag hanging off his shoulder, looking the total outcast. As an orphan and the town pariah, he had no one who would miss him here—but I was happy he'd be at my side for the rest of my life.

But then I caught sight of an unexpected face in the crowd, one that stood out with its mix of flaws and perfection. Roth pushed past people until he emerged in front of me, while people stared at his scarred face. It was rare for him to be out in public like this, especially in bright daylight.

"You're here," I said, breathless and afraid to hope that he'd changed his mind.

"I'm here," he said. "I couldn't let you choose some stranger to be your fourth. Though I'm not sure what use a fisherman will be at the Fire Temple."

I smiled at him, while resisting the urge to hug him in front of all these people, which I knew he'd hate. "Valefire is on the coast, and we'll still need to eat. Even if that weren't true, I'd want you with me anyway."

"I knew you'd change your mind," Derel said to Roth, who just scowled.

"We ready to get moving?" Blane asked.

"Don't rush her," Falon said.

Blane rolled his eyes. "I'm not, but if we want to make it to the temple by tomorrow night, we'll need to get on the road soon."

"I'm almost ready," I said, before turning back to my mother and sisters. Emotion clogged my chest and tears filled my eyes as I hugged them one by one.

"Good luck," Krea whispered in my ear.

"I'm going to miss you so much," Loka said.

My mother hugged me so long and tight I started to feel like she was never going to let me go. Then she pulled back to look at me. "This is your destiny and I'm very proud of you. Your father would be too. Take care of yourself and those four young men, and come visit whenever you can."

I sniffed. "I will."

"Remember, you're descended from a long line of priestesses." She patted my cheek. "Now get to the Fire Temple before the volcano tears apart our town."

I chuckled through my tears. "Yes, Mom."

I turned away and grabbed the bag that held the few things I'd decided to take with me. It was time to face my destiny.

My four men formed a circle around me as we moved through the town, parting the crowd like a wave. The people I'd known my entire life now looked at me with a mix of awe, fear, and hope. Many of them called out their blessings or wished us well, some even thanking us for protecting them from the volcano, while others frowned or turned away. Maybe they didn't believe the Fire God had truly chosen me, or maybe they didn't agree with me taking four mates.

"Whore," someone muttered in the crowd, and Blane lurched forward like he would strike the person down. Falon gripped his arm and held him back. I bowed my head, my face heating up and no doubt turning red, and picked up my pace. Though it was sad leaving my village and family, there were definitely some people I would not miss.

We kept walking and soon left the crowd and the town behind. I'd gone over the map with my mother last night, since she'd visited the Fire Temple once as a child, though she hadn't left Sparkport in many years. According to her, people in our village used to regularly visit the temple and leave offerings, but that fell out of practice. It was likely no one had visited for at least twenty years now.

As we followed the road, I hefted my bag higher on my shoulder. I'd only brought one, and it had been hard to leave a lifetime's worth of belongings behind, but for this journey I only needed the essentials. Plus a few books, of course. I would return and get the rest of my things once I was settled in the temple.

"Thank you again for coming with me," I said to the men, who had fanned out around me. "I know it was a lot to ask and on such short notice too. I mean, you had to give up your families, your professions, and your homes. I'm still in awe that you all said yes."

"You had to give up all of those things too when the Fire God chose you," Falon pointed out. "At least we had a choice."

"The Fire God did give me a choice, but it didn't feel like much of one. How do you say no to a God?" I smiled faintly as I remembered my fear upon meeting him. "Although I wouldn't have said no anyway. Though it was a shock at first, I truly feel this is my path. As if I'd been searching for myself my entire life and now I finally found her. And all of you are a part of that. Maybe there was a reason I felt so strongly for all of you..." I trailed off, stealing glances at the men, wondering if I'd said too much. I still didn't know if they felt the same for me. They were here with me, but was that because of duty, friendship, desire...or love?

"Anyway, I really appreciate that you're all going on this journey with me," I added quickly. "For the last few years I've been torn between each of you, unable to decide who I wanted to spend my life with. I'm so happy that now I don't have to decide. I can have you all."

Falon cleared his throat. "I can't speak for the others, but I'm happy to be here, even if it was unexpected."

"You know I'm always up for an adventure," Blane said.

"No kidding," Roth said. "Did you bring the fireworks?"

"Of course I did," Blane said.

Derel rolled his eyes. "You'll probably shoot off your arm with them."

Blane grinned. "If I do, we'll call it an offering to the Fire God. He'll love it."

I laughed and shook my head. If nothing else, I would never be bored at the Fire Temple with these four around.

It wasn't long before we had to diverge off the road to

begin walking on the rough terrain. The volcano was almost directly north of Sparkport on the coast, and while there might have been a road leading to it years ago, it had all but vanished now. This journey would have been a lot faster and easier if we were all riding horses, but our village didn't have any that could be spared. I wasn't sure we'd be able to get horses up the volcano anyway—we were in for a bit of a climb once we reached it.

I glanced up at Valefire in the distance, which was still releasing a never-ending stream of white smoke into the sky. Journeying there seemed an impossible task, and no one in their right mind would ever want to live there. I could only trust that the Fire God knew what he was doing—even if it was hard to banish my fears and doubts about what was to come.

CHAPTER EIGHT

We stopped for a quick lunch by a tiny stream that looked like it might dry up at any moment. How would we get water at the volcano anyway? People had lived there at one point so there must be a way, but it only reminded me I had no idea what to expect at the temple.

I sat with my back against a scraggly little tree which offered a tiny amount of shade. Derel sat beside me, taking the rest of the shade, while the other guys found other spots near the stream to try to stay cool. As we got closer to Valefire it would no doubt get hotter too.

"What do you think we'll encounter at the Fire Temple?" I asked, as I ripped apart a piece of the bread my mother had packed for us.

Derel brushed crumbs off of himself. "I don't know. Hopefully it's still standing."

"Were your parents upset about you leaving? They'll

have to find someone else to help run the butcher shop now."

"Dad was upset, but luckily my cousin can step in and take my place at the shop. Mom was sad, but was also excited because I was going with you." He rolled his eyes. "Still hoping we'll get married and give her tons of grand-kids, no doubt."

"Of course." Except...we kind of were getting married. Not officially, but in practice. Unless they didn't see it the same way I did?

"Are you sure you want to do this?" I asked, trying to ignore the tightness in my chest. "I know the two of us haven't always gotten along in the past."

He snorted. "Only because you're always picking fights with me."

I turned to face him. "Me? You're the one who is always rude to me!"

"Maybe because you deserve it."

I threw my last piece of bread at his head. "I do not. If anyone deserves rudeness, it's you."

He threw the bread back at me, his brows drawn together. "Gods, you make me crazy, Calla. You're stubborn and infuriating and so damn beautiful it nearly hurts to look at you sometimes."

"I...what?" I'd been so ready to argue with him more that his last words made my mouth fall open in shock.

He slid his hand into my hair and drew me toward him, capturing my wordless surprise with his lips. Twenty years of pent-up frustration and desire unraveled at his kiss and I found myself pulling at his shirt to draw him closer. When his tongue slid against mine it sent a rush of heat right between my legs.

"I'm shocked," I managed to say. "I had no idea you felt that way."

"Don't be ridiculous. You must know how we all feel about you."

"No, I truly don't." Although I was beginning to realize it. I probably should have known all along, but I'd been worried my feelings for them were mostly one-sided. Only once they'd agreed to journey with me to the Fire Temple did I realize they might care for me the same way I cared for them.

Derel ran his fingers through my blond hair like he couldn't get enough of it. "I've wanted to kiss you for years. I've spent long nights thinking about wrapping this hair around my fingers. And all the other things I want to do with you too..."

"If you had feelings for me, why didn't you ever tell me?

He shrugged. "I thought you hated me."

I softened against him and touched his face in wonder. "I never hated you, I just hated the circumstances we were in. Our mothers forced us together from the time we were born. We never had a choice in the matter and that made me frustrated. I guess I took it out on you. I'm sorry."

"I'm equally guilty. I was pretty horrible to you at times."

"Yes, like the time you pushed me in the ocean when we

were five. Or when we were seven and you tricked me into sitting on those strawberries and ruined my dress. Or—"

He grimaced. "Okay, yes, I was quite awful. But I had to get your attention somehow." He let out a low laugh. "Wow, I'd forgotten about the strawberries. No wonder you hated me."

"I didn't hate you. Well, maybe a little..."

He pulled me close and kissed me again, and every time it was like a revelation. I'd spent my entire life thinking Derel was my nemesis. Now I looked on him with a whole new light.

"We should probably get going," he finally said. He helped me to my feet and we brushed dirt off ourselves, but then he paused. "There was another reason I was rude to you."

"What was it?"

He glanced over at the other guys, who looked like they were trying to watch us without being too obvious about it. "Falon."

"Falon only sees me as a friend."

"We both know that's not true of anyone in this group." He shook his head. "Like I said last night, you should talk to him about that."

With those words he grabbed his pack and walked away, leaving me with only my thoughts. I grabbed my things and hurried after him.

For the next few hours we traveled through the empty wilds, the volcano looming large in front of us. As I kicked up dirt, I went through my memories of Derel and saw everything he'd done—all the pranks, the teasing, the arguments—in a new light. It made me wonder what else I'd been wrong about all my life.

I slowed my pace to fall in line with Falon, who walked at the rear of the group. Last time I'd tried to talk to Falon about us it hadn't gone as planned, but his being here had to be a sign he cared for me as more than a friend...didn't it?

"I see you and Derel have worked out your issues finally," he said with a teasing voice.

"We did." While Derel had long driven me mad, Falon had a way of calming me. I always relaxed in his presence. "He told me to talk to you."

He ducked his head and rubbed the back of his neck. "Me? Why?"

"He said one of the reasons he pushed me away all these years was because of you." I glanced over at Falon quickly to gauge his reaction, but couldn't meet his eyes.

He blew out a long breath. "What a pair we are. He wouldn't do anything because of me, and I wouldn't do anything because of him."

"What do you mean?"

He stopped and turned toward me, allowing me to gaze into his clear blue eyes. "Gods, after so many years this is difficult to finally admit. I have feelings for you, Calla. I always have."

Warmth spread throughout my chest. "Why didn't you tell me?"

"You've been promised to Derel for our entire lives—how was I supposed to get in the way of that?"

"You knew that was what our parents wanted, not us."

"Trust me, Derel wanted it too. He pretended he didn't because he knew how I felt about you and he didn't want to get in the way. Which naturally was the same reason I never acted on my feelings. Maybe one of us might have told you the truth eventually, but then you became involved with Roth and it looked like you would marry him, so we decided to keep our feelings to ourselves."

"Yes, but my relationship with Roth didn't last long."

"True, but then you started seeing Blane..."

I shook my head. "That wasn't serious."

He arched an eyebrow. "Is that what you think? Because I'm pretty sure it's serious to him."

I bit my lip and looked over at Blane. I'd have to talk to him later to see if Falon was right. I turned back to Falon and sighed. "I wish I'd known the truth all this time. I thought you only saw me as a friend."

"I didn't know if you felt that way for me either. Not until last night." He took my hands in his and gave me a warm smile. "I was terrified if I told you I had feelings for you that you wouldn't return them and it would ruin our friendship. I couldn't stand the thought of that. I tried to tell myself your friendship was enough, and that I'd be happy if you married one of the other guys, but the truth was, I was miserable seeing you with them. I wanted it to be me."

"Are you going to be okay with this arrangement?"

"I think so. It's the perfect solution." He glanced over at the other three guys, who were still trudging along ahead of us. "The five of us were all so close when we were younger.

We've each loved you for years. But we knew if we acted on it, it could tear our group apart."

"Roth and Blane acted on it," I pointed out.

"Roth was a selfish jerk before the attack," Falon said with a wink. "But we would have gladly let you marry him if he made you happy. Blane too, for that matter. But you probably noticed that once you became involved with them, the group stopped spending as much time together."

I nodded. "I know, and I realize that was partly my fault. I just hope this situation brings us closer together instead of tearing us further apart."

"It will. We may be hesitant at first to share you, but we'd rather share you than not have you at all." He took my face in his hands. "And now I'm going to kiss you, because I'm the only one who never has."

"Finally," I said.

He bent his head and touched his mouth to mine slowly, then gave me soft, teasing kisses, as though he was learning the shape of my lips. I slid my arms around his neck and pulled him closer, wanting more, but he was infuriatingly patient. I suppose he had to be, if he'd waited this long to kiss me. But then his tongue swiped across my lower lip and I opened for him with a gasp. As his tongue slid sensually against mine, he clutched me in his arms and made me feel cherished and adored, like he wanted to take his time kissing me and never let me go.

He pressed his forehead against mine. "Even better than I imagined it would be."

"Good, now you've kissed all of us," Blane called out. "We can finally move on to the fun stuff."

I laughed. "What makes you think that will happen?"

"A man can hope."

"That seems rather presumptuous," I said, as I hefted my bag onto my other shoulder and continued walking alongside Falon. Gods, why had I packed so many things? With each step the bag became heavier and heavier.

"Isn't that why we're here?" Blane asked with a wicked grin. "To serve you?"

"You're coming with me to serve the Fire God." A small smile played across my lips. "And to keep me company, I suppose."

"I think Blane has a specific way he wants to pass the time," Derel said.

Blane chuckled. "As if you aren't hoping for the same thing."

CHAPTER NINE

I thought about Blane's comment as we found a spot to make camp for the night. I had kissed all of them now, although I hadn't kissed Roth in years. Not since the night of the attack, when our lives changed forever. I wanted to kiss him again, but would he let me?

I'd tried to be supportive after his injury. I'd told him I didn't care what he looked like, that I loved him no matter what and still wanted to be with him—but he couldn't even listen to the words without going into a rage. He was in so much pain, both inside and out, and he said that seeing me only made it worse. He asked me to leave him alone, telling me he didn't want me anymore, and I foolishly listened, hoping he would change his mind once he healed. Now I wished I could go back and force myself to stay, no matter what harmful things he'd said to me.

It was warm enough that we didn't need a fire, but I

drifted away from the group and began practicing my new magic on some weeds growing up from some rocks. The fire came easier now, though it still surprised me every time.

"I thought only the Dragons had magic," Roth said, his gravelly voice behind me.

"Me too. It seems the Gods can make exceptions." I tried to snuff out the flames, but when my magic didn't work, I stomped on the weeds with my boots. "I'm sorry. Does the fire bring back bad memories?"

"It's fine. We should get back to the camp though."

I nodded and began to follow him, but then stopped. I was tired of this distance between us. "Roth, wait."

He stopped and turned toward me, the moonlight highlighting both halves of his face. It made my chest tighten with emotion, and I found myself crossing the distance to him. When he didn't move away, I gripped his shirt in my hand and lifted on my toes to press my mouth against his. At first he didn't respond and I worried I'd made a fool of myself, but then he let out a groan and his arms went around me, hauling me against his muscular body. His mouth devoured mine like he was making up for the last two years.

My back pressed against the boulder behind me as Roth's lips trailed down my neck. Desire swept through me, hot and needy, and I fumbled for his trousers, wanting him inside me again. Gods, it had been way too long, and I'd never stopped aching for him since that night.

He tore his mouth from mine as my fingers rubbed against his hard bulge. "Calla... We shouldn't."

"Why not? We've slept together before."

"Yes, but not since *this.*" He gestured at the burn marring his otherwise perfect face.

"I don't care about that. I loved you before your scars and I love you now too. If they took over your entire body I would still love you." He didn't say anything as I took his face in my hands. "Besides, this side of you is so pretty you need something to balance it out. Otherwise you'd make the other guys jealous."

That finally got one corner of his mouth to twitch up. "I *was* always the best looking one in our group."

I pressed a kiss to both of his cheeks. "I was so happy when I saw you in the crowd this morning. I couldn't imagine spending my life without you. And now we're here together, and I'm ready to go back to what we once had."

He let out a ragged breath. "I love you too, Calla."

My eyes widened. "You do?"

"I should have said it years ago. I just couldn't imagine you would still love me when I looked like this, especially when you almost died that night. I figured if I stayed away, you'd marry one of the other guys, who I knew also loved you."

"They were probably worried about hurting you by being with me."

"Maybe, though I did a pretty good job of pushing them away over the years. Especially Blane." He tangled his fingers in my hair. "I was both relieved and jealous when the two of you started seeing each other. I hoped you would be happy together."

"I didn't think it was serious with Blane, but now I'm starting to wonder. And I never slept with him, you know."

"No? What about the others?"

"You're my first and only."

His grip on my hair tightened, turning possessive as he looked down at me with hunger. "You're my first and only too. Although I suspect I won't be your only much longer."

"Does that bother you?"

"No. I lost my claim on you years ago." He glanced back at the camp. "And maybe we all knew, deep down, this was the only way for us to all be happy."

"I think I knew that too. I was just afraid to admit it, and I worried what people would think of us."

"Now you don't have to worry."

"No, I don't." I slid my hands into his thick hair to pull him close again. "But at this moment I only want you."

His mouth crushed against mine and he pressed me back against the boulder. I wrapped myself tighter around him and his hands slid down to cup my behind, lifting me up and against him. My skirts bunched up around my hips and I wrapped my legs around him, marveling at his strong shoulders, built from working long hours on the docks and on his uncle's fishing boat. I'd spent a lot of time at the docks watching him, both before and after his injury, staring at his shirtless body as he hauled on ropes and climbed the rigging of his uncle's ship, remembering what it felt like to touch that tanned skin. The same skin I was touching and tasting now.

Passion and desire made us desperate for each other.

With one hand pressed against the boulder for support, he used his other hand to pull open his trousers. I gasped as the head of his cock pushed against my core, which was already so wet for him. I'd been waiting to feel him inside me again for years, and I tightened my legs around him, not wanting to delay another second. His fingers gripped my behind as he entered me nice and slow, filling me up completely and making me stretch around him. Gods, I'd forgotten how big he was and how good he felt inside me.

He began to move with deep, languid strokes that hit me in all the right places. I clung to his neck as his strong arms held us up, the hard stone digging into my back while he pumped into me. He captured my mouth again and the touch of his tongue against mine made me nearly come undone. I'd waited so long to be one with him again, and now I never wanted it to end.

But he demanded more, pushing me further, shifting me higher, until the angle of his movements was just perfect. I was close, so close, and as his lips trailed across my neck I let go, giving in to the sweet friction of our bodies and his hard length filling me. My head fell back as sensation washed over me and I pulsed around him, nails digging into his shoulders as I called out his name. He rewarded me by thrusting harder and faster until he released himself inside me with a throaty groan.

I pressed my forehead against his as we trembled together, overcome with the emotions coursing through us. Soon our lips found each other again, but this time we kissed slowly, our movements unhurried. As if we only now realized we had the rest of our lives to do this again and again. Now that we'd found each other a second time, there was no need to rush.

But then I remembered the other men back in camp. They probably had a good idea of what we were doing, and I couldn't help but wonder what they thought about it. Would they be jealous...or would they want to join in?

CHAPTER TEN

I woke to find a strong arm wrapped around me, holding me close. For a moment I simply reveled in the feeling of a large, masculine body at my back and the mystery man's even breathing in my ear. I wasn't sure who it was, but it didn't matter, because I would gladly wake up beside any one of my men...or all of them.

When Roth and I had returned last night, the other men had been quiet. Falon and Derel would barely meet my eyes, while Blane openly grinned at me. I'd been completely exhausted at that point, and had practically fallen onto my bedroll and passed out immediately. It seemed someone had joined me in the middle of the night.

I must have stirred a little, because I felt his breathing change as he woke. Warm lips pressed a kiss to my neck and the arm tightened around me.

"Morning, beautiful," Blane drawled.

I should have known it was him. None of the other men would have been so bold. I turned my head just enough to catch his mouth and draw him into a kiss without a word. I'd wanted to sleep with Blane for a long time, but I'd always held back because I was never sure if what we had together was real. Once he'd volunteered to go with me to the Fire Temple, I'd realized I'd misjudged him, along with our relationship. And now that I'd had a reminder of how good sex could be, I wanted to experience it with Blane too.

Judging by the hardness pressed against my behind, he wanted me just as badly. I rubbed back against him and he groaned, then slid his hand down my chemise to cup my breast. His thumb flicked over my hard nipple, while his mouth found my neck and pressed a warm kiss there.

"You've tempted me for so long," his rough voice said in my ear. "Last night I heard your moans of pleasure with Roth, and now *I'm* going to be the one making you moan."

"Yes," I managed to whisper.

His fingers trailed down and down, reaching the bottom of my chemise, which he yanked up enough to gain access to my naked body underneath. His hand roamed across my skin as he explored me, and I wished I could touch him more too, but at the same time I loved the way he was in control. When that hand finally slid between my thighs, I cried out for more.

He traced my folds and made a soft humming sound of approval. "So wet for me already?"

"Blane, please," I whispered, trying to keep my voice

down to not wake the others in the camp. I had a feeling that wouldn't last long though.

He hooked my leg back over his and then his cock nudged between my thighs from behind. With one smooth thrust he was inside, filling me up completely. Gods, he was huge and so thick too. His fingers dug into my hip while he slid deep, over and over again, and all I could do was gasp with each stroke. I spread myself wider, pushing back against him in time with his movements, trying to take as much of him as possible.

He claimed me with each thrust, and then his fingers slid between my thighs too. I turned my head back toward him and he took my mouth in a deep, rough kiss while he continued pumping in and out of me. Our bodies moved together in a delicious rhythm, faster and faster, until it became too much. Pleasure crept over me in rolling waves and I tore my mouth away from him to cry out his name. His fingers kept up their pressure and urged me into new heights, while he pinned me back against him. With a rough growl he pushed deep and held me there as his cock pulsed inside me with his release.

For some time we simply lay there, entwined together in blissful silence, until our breathing calmed. I turned back toward him with a smile, amazed he was here with me. Of all the men, I'd figured he would say no to my offer—but instead he'd been the first to volunteer.

"I can't see you being a priest somehow," I said.

"Yeah, me neither. Truthfully I don't care about any of that stuff. The Gods can rot for all I care. I'm only here for you." He pressed a kiss to my neck. "Besides, my family is gone and Sparkport never accepted me. I would have left years ago and never returned if not for you."

I rolled over to face him, surprised by his confession. "I was never sure if you truly cared for me in that way, or if I was just a temporary distraction before you went off on some adventure again."

"I always came back, didn't I?"

"Yes, but I figured you had women in other towns..." I shrugged.

"I did when you and Roth were together. When that ended, I decided I only wanted you."

"Why didn't you tell me?"

"Because I knew you'd never want to be with me, not like that. You worried about what people would think of us being together." I opened my mouth to protest but he silenced me with a kiss. "Admit it, you were."

"Only because I knew my mother would never let me marry you." My eyes dropped. "Maybe there is some truth to what you are saying. I'm sorry. I shouldn't have let that come between us."

"And I should have been clear that I wanted you for more than just a little fun on the side." He cupped my cheek and gazed into my eyes. "I've always loved you. I just never thought I would ever be lucky enough to have you. I certainly don't deserve you."

"I love you too," I said, before pressing another kiss to his lips. "And don't say that. You were the first to volunteer to go with me."

"The others have families and homes and professions to leave behind. I had nothing, except you." He drew me tighter into his arms. "You're all that matters to me."

"If you two lovebirds are done, it's time we get going," Derel called out.

Blane chuckled. "He must be jealous."

Was he? If the other men were jealous or upset, I'd have to find a way to fix that soon. We were going to spend the rest of our lives together, the five of us in one small temple, and I'd have to make sure we were all okay with that—and everything it entailed.

CHAPTER ELEVEN

The closer we got to the volcano the more desolate the landscape became. The ground under our feet became black from ancient lava now hardened, and plumes of steam and boiling water would sometimes burst up without warning. The air grew hotter too, and began to smell of burning weeds and rotten eggs. Valefire raged on without care, sending white smoke up into the air and making the land rumble beneath us, and all I could do was trust that the Fire God would keep his end of the bargain.

Once we reached the base of Valefire, we were all covered in a thin layer of ash and sweat, and now came the hard part—the climb. We took a quick break to drink water and eat some of the sliced pork Derel had brought, gathering our strength as best we could before the final part of our journey.

"Do you think it will erupt?" Falon asked, as he wiped sweat off his brow.

"Not if we make it there soon," I said, hoping I was right. I straightened up again and hefted my bag over my shoulder with a groan. At first it had seemed far too small considering all the things I'd left behind, but now it felt like a load of bricks on my back. I started to wish I'd been even more selective when I'd packed.

“Here, let me help you with that,” Falon said, as he reached for my bag.

“Oh. Thank you.” I rolled my shoulders with relief.

He threw my bag onto his back. “Gods, this thing must weigh a ton. What do you have in here?”

“My clothes and some other things.”

“And a stack of books, no doubt,” Roth said.

“I only brought a few!” It had made me sick leaving any of my books behind, but I couldn’t exactly carry them all.

“How many is a few?” Derel asked.

I bit my lip. “Um, four?”

Falon laughed. “Four? No wonder this thing is so heavy.”

“If we divide them up between all of us it won’t be so bad,” Derel said.

“All right, but I’m carrying my bag again after that,” I said, as I took it back from Falon and opened it up. I handed each of the guys one of my small leather-bound books, and they slipped them into their own packs. Except for Blane, who stared at his.

"This is the one I got you," he said. "You brought it with you."

"Of course I did. It's my favorite." Blane had picked up the book on one of his journeys to the Air Realm, which was known for its amazing libraries and museums.

He opened his mouth, but no words came out. When he looked up at me, emotion flickered across his face. "Why?"

"Because it came from you." I leaned close and pressed a quick kiss to his lips, while the other guys watched.

Blane pulled me closer and pressed his lips to my ear. "I love you."

I nuzzled my face in his neck. I should have realized the true depth of Blane's feelings when he got me the book, but it was nice to have no doubts about them now. "I love you too."

We broke apart and began to ascend the mountain. The climb was grueling, especially when we were already exhausted. The hot sun on our backs didn't help, nor did the thick layer of smoke as we got higher and higher. I coughed constantly and felt like I would never be clean again, assuming I could make it to the summit without passing out. The men didn't seem to be faring much better, and would often stop to readjust their bags or wipe sweat from their brows. The relentless heat and the horrible smells only made it worse. Would we ever get used to this?

When we finally reached the summit, my knees were weak and I could barely find the strength to stand. But there, rising before us, was the temple of the Fire God in all its glory—our new home.

The temple was a large building made entirely of obsidian, the black volcanic glass so common in this part of the Fire Realm. In Sparkport we used it for many things—arrowheads, tools, jewelry—and many traders sold it in other parts of the world. But I'd never seen an entire structure made out of it.

Night had fallen sometime during our ascent, and the black temple was highlighted from behind by the eerie orange glow from the great open maw of the volcano.

"We're here," Roth said. "Now what?"

I hesitated. "I suppose we go inside and make ourselves at home."

Derel and Falon moved to the great temple door and tugged it open with some difficulty. As they did, a rush of dust fluttered out into the humid air. The room inside was pitch black, and I summoned a ball of flame into my palm as we stepped inside.

With the feeble light shining inside the expansive room, I caught sight of something. A flash of light and dark. A whisper of movement. A hint we weren't alone.

I gripped Blane's arm. "What was that?"

"I didn't see anything," he said, although he drew his sword anyway.

"It looked like a shadow," Falon said with a frown.

"Rats probably," Derel added.

I nodded and continued forward, tampering down my fear while moving across the stone floor. I made the flame bigger to illuminate more of the room, and gasped at what the light revealed.

Shadowy figures with dimly glowing eyes stood around the great hall. They looked almost like humans except for their long claws and the way their bodies tapered off near the bottom. As those glowing yellow eyes turned toward us, cold fear shot down my spine.

"Shades," Blane said, as he pushed me behind him.

Impossible. Shades were a myth, nothing more. They were stories parents told to their children to keep them from misbehaving. Shades were said to once have been friendly spirits, but were now twisted, deadly ghosts trapped between this world and the next. Worst of all, they were hungry...and nearly impossible to kill.

The shades rushed toward us, trailing across the floor with their insubstantial bodies, moving through anything in their way. Roth, Derel, and Falon all drew their weapons too, swiping at the nearest ones alongside Blane. Each of the men knew how to fight, while all I could do was stand behind them and pray. Except their blades went straight through the shades as if they were nothing but air.

“Weapons don’t hurt them!” Derel called out.

“We need fire,” Roth said, as one of the shades tried to claw at his arm.

Fire—of course. Like the elementals, shades could probably only be stopped by fire, water, air, or earth.

That meant I had to do something, but how? I wasn't a fighter. I'd never killed anyone before. But we were in danger and I couldn’t let my men get injured. I summoned the Fire God’s gift into my palms, the heat giving me clarity and strength. As the shade lunged for Roth again, I threw my ball of fire at it. The magic hit with a loud sizzle and flames flashed all over the shade, before the creature vanished in a cloud of black smoke. I felt a split second of triumph, before more shades crowded around us.

Now that we'd seen what my fire could do to the shades, I summoned even more of it. Blane grabbed a torch off the wall and swept it through my ball of flame, lighting it instantly. Falon picked up a discarded chair and broke it over his knee, splintering the wood into pieces. He tossed them to Derel and Roth, and they gestured for me to light their stakes as well. Roth hesitated as his stake lit up with fire, no doubt remembering how he got his injury, but then he guarded me from the shades with the others.

We backed up behind a discarded bookshelf and some tables, but the shades moved right through the furniture without slowing at all. Blane rushed the closest one with a roar, swiping his torch at it. The other shades surrounded us almost instantly, and I could barely summon fire fast enough to blast them before they got to me. The men fought them off with their improvised fiery weapons, although the shades' claws still managed to rip through their clothes and slash their skin.

As another of my men cried out, fear swelled within me and I prayed to the Fire God for help. We were in his temple, doing his work, why wasn't he helping us? Was this some kind of test? Were we on our own?

But he'd given me a gift, and even though I barely knew how to control it, I felt it flickering inside me. My fear and determination to protect my mates only made it flare hotter, and I let out a roar and spread my arms, calling forth the Fire God's wrath with power I didn't know I possessed. Each shade in the room suddenly burnt up with a piercing scream, turning to ash.

As the power left me, I crumpled to the floor, completely spent. Derel rushed over to me and asked, "Are you all right?"

I nodded. "Yes, although it seems I need a little more practice with my magic."

The other men were immediately at my side, though they were all bleeding from various minor cuts from the shades. I was just relieved we were still alive.

Blane brushed back a damp piece of blond hair from my eyes. "I think you did a damn good job with your magic already."

"You were incredible," Falon said, touching my cheek lovingly.

Roth suddenly swept me up into his strong arms. "Let's find you somewhere to lie down."

"Really, I'm fine," I said, though I didn't protest too much because I liked being held like this against his hard body.

He grunted and carried me through the dark temple, while the others lit torches where we could find them to brighten the dark halls. The room with the shades had been some sort of grand entrance hall, with tall ceilings and a huge statue of a fiery dragon in the center. Other doors led down hallways to more rooms, including kitchens, store-rooms, bedrooms, and washrooms. Tomorrow I wanted to fully explore, but at the moment it took everything I had to keep my eyes open.

I barely remembered Roth setting me down, or the others tucking some blankets over me. All I knew was that each one kissed me goodnight, and I fell asleep wondering if this would ever feel like home.

CHAPTER TWELVE

In the morning I discovered I'd been placed in a bedroom that the men had prepared for me, although it needed more cleaning, as did the rest of the temple. Dim, murky light shone through the windows from the smoke-covered sky, reminding me that the volcano still raged on. We'd made it to the temple—would the Fire God speak to me soon and tell me my purpose?

I visited the washroom quickly, then began a more thorough tour of the temple. I barely remembered anything from last night after the shade attack, and now I surveyed the building with a more critical eye, making a mental note of everything I'd want to change or fix. Though the temple itself was all black volcanic stone and didn't need any repairs, everything inside it required straightening, repairing, or cleaning. If we were going to live here for the rest of our lives, we had a lot of work to do.

I stopped in the kitchen, where Derel was scrubbing down the counters. "I had a feeling you'd be in here."

He looked up at me with a wry grin. "Someone needs to cook for us. Unless you want to do it?"

I held up my hands in surrender. "I'll help with the baking if you'd like, but you're welcome to take over in the kitchen. That was more my sisters' area of expertise."

"Yes, I remember." He propped his hip on the counter and offered me a bit of bread, ham, and cheese. "You preferred to hole up in a corner somewhere with your books."

"That's true," I said, as I devoured the food. When was the last time I'd eaten? Lunch yesterday, perhaps? "Unfortunately I couldn't turn reading into a profession."

"You can now."

"What do you mean?"

Amusement made his dark eyes dance. "Let's just say you're going to be very happy when you see the library."

My eyes widened. "There's a library?"

He nodded. "I'm pretty sure it has more books than all of Sparkport. It'll take you years to read them all."

I finished off his food and wiped my hands. "I'd better get started then."

"Not yet," he said, taking my arm. "There's another place I think you'll want to visit first."

"What is it?"

"I'll show you."

He led me out of the kitchen and down the halls. I spotted Roth and Blane arranging some furniture in another room, but Derel continued on. Soon we came upon a cave-like room filled with steaming water in a few different pools. Falon was already inside and turned toward us with a smile.

"What is this place?" I asked.

"A natural hot spring," Falon said, as he bent down to dip his fingers in. He brought them to his lips with a smile. "Freshwater. Nice and warm too."

"This is where we'll get our water to drink and cook with," Derel said, gesturing at one of the smaller pools, before turning to the largest one. "And this one can be used for bathing."

"Incredible." I wanted to fall to my knees and thank the Fire God for providing this for us. I'd suspected there was a way to survive up here, but this was better than I'd imagined.

Derel moved behind me and began sliding down the straps of my dress. "I think we should try it out."

"Do you?" I asked, my breath catching as he pressed a kiss to my neck.

Falon closed in on me from the front, caging me between his best friend. "You must be eager to wash off the dirt from our days of traveling." His hands slid along my bare arms as his mouth lowered to mine. "We can help."

"I am feeling quite dirty," I said, before our lips met.

Derel left a trail of kisses down my neck to my shoulder, then tugged my dress down, revealing one of my breasts. Falon immediately palmed it in his large, rough hand, and began squeezing my flesh. I moaned as Derel continued yanking the dress down, freeing another breast for his friend to claim. The fabric brushed against my hips as my entire torso was bared to the two men, who took their time exploring me with eager strokes and light kisses.

Their boldness surprised and thrilled me. Derel and I hadn't gotten along for most of my life, but the sexual chemistry had always simmered between us under the surface. Now that he'd admitted his feelings for me, it seemed he didn't want to hold back any longer. Falon, on the other hand, had always acted as though he was nothing more than a friend, but not anymore. As he took one breast in his mouth and ran his tongue over my nipple, I didn't have any more doubts that what we had was more than friendship.

"We know you've been with Blane and Roth, but now we're going to make you ours," Derel's voice said, as he nipped at my ear. His hard length pressed against my behind and sent a rush of wet heat between my thighs.

Falon ran his hand down my hips to continue easing my dress down, until it fell to the floor. "For years we held back because of our friendship, knowing we could never be happy if you picked one of us. But that isn't a problem anymore."

"I want you both," I said, pressing a kiss to Falon's lips, before turning to kiss Derel too. "I've always wanted you both."

"How about at the same time?" Derel asked, as he stroked my behind.

"Is that possible?"

"Oh yes." He gave my bottom a hard squeeze. "Now get in the water."

The two men watched as I moved toward the spring and

stepped down into the water. Delicious warmth crept over me as I sank into it, making all my muscles relax. Before me, both men began to undress, tearing off their shirts and dropping their trousers, revealing their muscular bodies and jutting cocks. If this was going to be my life from now on, I couldn't complain.

Derel descended first into the water and took me in his arms, kissing me hard while his fingers slipped between my thighs. He stroked me in both my mouth and my core and I had to cling to him as pleasure swept over me. His wet, muscular body pressed against mine in the most sensual way, and I wrapped my legs around him to get even closer. His cock slipped inside me as we came together, like it couldn't help but find its way to where it belonged. I gasped at the sudden joining, but then his tongue was sliding against mine, matching his thrusts.

Then Falon's hands were on me too, his body fitted against my back. He was even more muscular than Derel from days spent working as a carpenter, and I enjoyed the feel of his hard ridges on my skin. Along with the other hard thing poking into my behind, which I knew wanted a taste of me too.

While Derel gripped my hips to pump into me, Falon's hands claimed my breasts and his mouth sucked on my neck. I arched back against him, taking Derel deeper, while turning my head to capture Falon's mouth. Derel leaned down to lick water off my neck, but then he pulled out of me and spun me toward Falon. With water churning around us, Falon took me into his arms and captured my mouth, then entered me with one smooth push. He filled me up just as well as Derel did, but it was different. Derel was longer, but Falon was thicker—and both of them were mine.

"I think we're clean enough," Derel said.

Falon nodded and lifted me out of the water, my body wrapped around him as he moved onto the black stone floor. He set me down on a long cloth the men had laid out, and then pumped into me from above a few times, like he couldn't help himself, before rolling us over so that I was on top. I took a moment to savor how huge he felt in this position, while Derel moved behind us. He picked up a bottle of oil, and I realized they'd been planning this all along. Waiting for me to wake up, so they could lay their claim to me...together.

Derel kneeled behind me and began stroking my behind, spreading my cheeks, sliding his oiled fingers along my back entrance. I gasped with each touch, especially as Falon slowly rocked underneath me. When Derel's finger eased inside, I let out a cry of pleasure and surprise. No one had touched me there before, and I was shocked to find how much I enjoyed it.

Derel spent a few minutes stretching me wide while I rode Falon, and it was hard to believe anything could be more pleasurable than this moment, but I knew it would be once Derel was inside me too.

Then Derel's fingers vanished, and were quickly replaced by something much larger, harder, and thicker. As he pushed inside my tight hole, a mix of pleasure and pain shot through me and I clung to Falon as I cried out. He held me in his arms and stroked my breasts lovingly, and when his mouth captured mine, Derel was able to inch deeper inside me from behind.

"That's it," he said. "Just relax and let me in."

"Oh Gods," I said, as he filled me up slowly, stretching me around him in impossible ways.

"You're doing great," Falon said, with a slight pinch to my nipples.

Suddenly Derel was all the way inside, his hips flush with my behind, and I drew in a ragged breath as the feelings swept through me. I was one with both men at the same time, all of us joined together in the most intimate way.

"Please," I dug my fingers into the light curls on Falon's chest and whimpered, not knowing what I asked for, only that I needed *more*.

Falon gripped my hips and began to thrust up into me, which made Derel move too. Derel's hands found my breasts and he arched over me from behind as he sank deep inside. Together the two of them began to move in a smooth rhythm, which felt more incredible than anything I'd ever known before. I was pressed between them, joined with them both, and all I could do was let them take control of my body and bring us all to release.

The climax swept through me quickly, making me cry out again and again as pleasure shook my body. I tightened up around both men and they seemed to surge inside me, both of them groaning and exploding together. All of us succumbing at the same time to the unimaginable pleasure of being one with each other's bodies.

As satisfaction swept over us, the men wrapped me in their arms, squeezing me between them, while they whispered that they loved me and always would. I whispered that I loved them too as I snuggled close against them, my enemy and my best friend, and thought how lucky I was to have them here with me.

CHAPTER THIRTEEN

After my tryst with Falon and Derel I found the library, while the men continued working in other rooms of the temple. At first all I could do was stare at the bookshelves lining every wall from floor to ceiling, full of dusty old tomes I couldn't wait to crack open. Then I slowly stepped inside, examining a seating area on one side of the room and a small desk on the other with a giant flame carved into it. This was all for me, the High Priestess, I realized. Maybe I was meant to be a scholar of sorts after all.

A faded leather journal sat on top of the desk, covered in dust. I blew it off as I sat in the chair and then flipped the journal open, the pages making an audible crack as they moved for the first time in years. With my breath in my throat, I began to read.

My name is Ara and one day I'm going to be the next High Priestess.

Ara—my grandmother! Did she leave this here for me? No, she couldn't have known I would come to the temple… but maybe she knew *someone* would.

For years the Dragons have been pressuring all the High Priestesses to step down. They're scared of what we know. They're afraid of what will happen if the Gods awaken.

My mother refuses to leave, of course, even though the Gods remain as dormant as this volcano. I've decided to record my thoughts in case something should happen to us, in the hopes that one day a future High Priestess will find it.

My mother said she didn't know why Ara had left the temple and moved to Sparkport. Could this journal hold the key? Was it because of the Dragons?

I'd lived in fear of the Dragons all my life, as did everyone else with any sense. But the Dragons served the Gods alongside the priests—didn't they? Why would they be afraid if the Gods woke? I had much to learn, obviously. Yet the Fire God remained silent.

I intended to read the journal cover to cover to learn about my grandmother's life and my role here, but for now I skipped to the very last entry, desperate to know why she'd left the temple.

Once I turned twenty I was supposed to leave the temple and find four priests who would become my mates. Instead I let the Crimson Dragon seduce me, much to my mother's dismay. She says he did it as a way to ruin me, and I suppose she might be right. If so, his plan worked—because I am pregnant.

I sat back and rested a hand over my racing heart. Gods,

was I the granddaughter of the Crimson Dragon? Sark was the most ruthless and brutal Dragon of them all, even though he served the Fire God and ostensibly protected the Fire Realm and led our armies. I'd only seen him a few times when he'd come to check on Sparkport to instill fear in us, and he had been quite handsome, especially for someone hundreds of years old. But I'd also heard rumors that he burnt down the houses of anyone he suspected of conspiring against the Dragons. How could my grandmother sleep with him?

I forced myself to keep reading the final entry.

Sark took advantage of me when I was young, lonely, and foolish...and now I'll never be able to convince four men to become my mates. Not when I am carrying another man's child—especially the Crimson Dragon's. I suspect that was his plan all along, to prevent me from becoming High Priestess, though now he has abandoned me, claiming the child cannot be his because he is loyal to the Black Dragon. No doubt she would punish all of us if she found out he had sired a child with someone else, which is why I must keep this secret to my grave.

My mother says that one day the Fire God will awaken and the next Black Dragon will be crowned. I'd hoped that I would be the High Priestess at the time, but Valefire remains silent and the Dragons continue to rule. I can no longer hold onto the hope that the Fire God will return from his slumber during my lifetime, and have decided to leave the temple and return to Sparkport to raise my child among my cousins. Perhaps it is for the best, as I find my faith lacking these days and have become a disappointment to my mother and those in the temple.

I can only pray that one of my descendants will find their way back to this temple when the Fire God awakens to carry out our divine mission, even though I have failed as High Priestess. If that is who is reading this, please accept my apology for not preparing you better. I had no idea if this day would ever come, but I trust you will make the Fire God proud.

And remember this above all else: we serve the Gods, not the Dragons.

I reread her words over and over as I absorbed everything she'd written. I was descended from both the High Priestess and the Crimson Dragon. I'd always thought the Dragons serve the Gods, but it seemed there was some conflict between them. Now that the Fire God had awakened, would the Dragons become our enemies?

Falon appeared in the doorway, breathing quickly. "Calla, there's something you need to see."

"What is it?"

"The Dragons are coming."

CHAPTER FOURTEEN

I rushed to the front of the temple with Falon, where the other men were already waiting and watching the sky. As I lifted my eyes, I caught sight of four large reptilian forms with massive wings and terrifying talons descending toward us quickly. With his blood red scales I spotted the Crimson Dragon immediately, leading the charge to his own temple. Beside him was the Golden Dragon, who represented the Air God; the Azure Dragon, who spoke for the Water God; and the Jade Dragon, who was meant to serve the Earth God. The Black Dragon, the avatar of the Spirit Goddess, was the only one missing, for which I was thankful. She was their leader and the most powerful and terrifying of them all.

As the Crimson Dragon landed on the temple's shiny black steps, his body transformed back into a man, and I stood face to face with my grandfather. His hair was a shockingly pale color, almost white, and cut in a short military style. I recognized my own brown eyes on him, though his were harsh as they swept over me with a scowl. As we stared at each other, I could tell he knew who I was. But before either of us could speak, the other Dragons touched the ground and shifted back to their human forms.

I'd never seen the others before. Doran, the Azure Dragon, had long golden hair, a rugged beard, and tanned, weathered skin. Beside him, Isen, the Golden Dragon, looked completely opposite with pale, perfect skin and shiny black hair tied back. The final Dragon, Heldor, had a shaved head and tattoos running down his muscular arms, his massive body an imposing figure even beside the other large men.

"It's true then," Heldor said, his voice low and rumbling. "The Fire God is free."

Doran arched an eyebrow. "How can we be sure? All I see is a bit of smoke."

Isen snorted. "The volcano hasn't been active all this time. Why else would it suddenly stir now?"

I remembered Ara's words. *They're afraid of what will happen if the Gods awaken.* I stepped forward and said, "The Fire God remains absent, my lords. It is only us here at the temple."

From the corner of my eye I saw my mates shift and cast strange glances at me, but they didn't know what I'd found. They hadn't read my grandmother's journal, or seen her warning. *We serve the Gods, not the Dragons.*

I wasn't sure what was happening, but I knew in my gut

that I must lie to the Dragons and protect the Fire God and whatever he had planned. He'd awakened and brought us here for a reason, and I had a feeling the Dragons wouldn't like it.

"Who is this?" Isen asked, casting a dismissive glance at me.

Sark pinned me with his cruel gaze. "The High Priestess."

"I thought this temple was abandoned," Heldor said, raising an eyebrow at Sark.

"It was."

I swallowed. "I'm trying to revive the old traditions in the hopes it will calm the volcano. It's been rumbling for some time, though my mother says that is normal."

"Has the Fire God spoken to you?" Heldor asked.

"No," I lied.

"Why should we believe you?" Isen asked, before his eyes fell on my mates. "Maybe we should make sure she's telling the truth."

"You think this girl could have awakened the Fire God?" Doran asked, with a haughty laugh. "Even if she did, the others are still bound. He is powerless on his own."

"I wouldn't call a God powerless," Isen snapped.

"We're wasting time here," Doran said. "I don't see any evidence of the Fire God. And Sark would know if he'd broken free, wouldn't he?"

Sark grunted in response, still staring at me in a way that made my skin crawl.

"This is your temple," Heldor said to Sark. "Find out the

truth and deal with it. Or Nysa will be forced to come here herself, and you know how she'll feel about that."

With that, Heldor shifted back into his dragon form, his dark green wings glimmering under the sun as he leaped into the air. Though I was sweating, a chill ran through me at his words. Nysa, the Black Dragon, rarely left the city of Soulspire where she ruled, but when she did, destruction and death followed.

"Return when you have answers," Isen told Sark, before his golden scales flashed bright as he took off toward the sky.

Sark grumbled and pushed his way past me inside the temple, leaving me alone with the Azure Dragon. The golden-haired man gave me a quick nod, before shifting and flying off, his glimmering dark blue body quickly blending in with the sky.

"What was that about?" Derel asked, once they were gone.

"I'll tell you later," I said. "For now, just follow my lead."

The other guys nodded and we headed back inside the temple to find Sark. He'd opened the door at the back of the great room, which had been locked up until now. It led to another room with a large bed on a raised platform, almost like an altar. The room was coated in a layer of dust and I got the sense it was meant for some kind of ritual. How odd.

Another door on the other side opened to the outside, behind the temple. I stepped through it and was hit with a wave of heat coming from the mouth of the volcano, which was only a short distance away.

Sark stood over the edge of it, looking down into the

smoking abyss. He spun around to face me as I approached. "Tell me the truth. Why are you here?"

I bowed my head. "I serve the Gods, as do you. Isn't that right?"

His lips pressed into a tight line. "Of course. That's why I must know if he's been freed."

I tilted my head. "I didn't realize the Fire God was imprisoned."

He grabbed my chin in his hand. "I can make you talk, you know. I'll burn off your limbs. Throw your mates into the pit. Turn your entire village to ash. Unless you tell me the truth."

"You would truly harm your own granddaughter?" I asked, keeping my voice sweet, even though I was more scared than I'd ever been in my life.

Behind me, my mates gasped, but Sark's eyes only narrowed. "You don't know what you speak of."

As his fingers tightened painfully on my chin, I met his gaze without flinching. "I wonder what the Black Dragon would say if she knew you had a child with someone else?"

He glared at me for a few more seconds, then shoved me away so hard I hit the ground, scraping my palms on the black rocks. Sark then turned to my mates and gave them all a dangerous look. They each stood poised to fight, even though there was no way any of them could win against Sark, the deadliest of the Black Dragon's mates.

"If the Fire God awakens, I expect you to send word to me immediately," he snapped.

I bowed low. "Of course. I live to serve the Dragons."

"See that you do, or everyone you love will suffer for it."

Sark's body seamlessly shifted into his terrifying dragon form before he launched into the air and flew over the mouth of the volcano. He let out a huge blast of fire as a warning, before he flew away.

Once he was only a tiny speck in the distance, my shoulders finally relaxed. The other men all surrounded me and wrapped their arms around me.

"Are you okay?" Falon asked.

I nodded. "I think so."

"What was that about?" Blane asked.

"Let's go inside," I said. "I have a lot to tell you."

But as we headed back toward the temple, the volcano began to rumble loudly and the ground shook beneath our feet. The air suddenly became much hotter, to the point where it became hard to breathe, and my skin tingled with awareness. As we turned back to the gaping maw, lava and sparks shot out from it as a monstrously large dragon reared up from inside it. This one was much larger and more incredible than the ones we'd just faced, and its skin seemed to be made from lava itself.

"Calla of the Fire Realm," the dragon's deep voice said, while it pinned me with its fiery eyes. "You have served me well."

"The Fire God," Falon whispered, while the ground continued to rumble around us.

"It's really true," Blane said, while Roth and Derel could only gape and stare in awe.

This must be the Fire God's true form, only seen here at

his most holy place. I bowed my head low, while the volcano surged around us. "I've done everything you asked. I came to the temple and brought four men to serve as my mates. Will you calm the volcano now?"

In response, the glow from the mouth of the volcano dimmed and the ground stopped shaking. "Very well. But there is still more for you to do."

I swallowed and glanced at the men at my side, who nodded and gazed back at me with determined eyes. "What would you have us do?"

"You must prepare for the next Dragons to rise—the ascendants."

I tilted my head, unsure if I'd heard him correctly. "The next ones?"

"The Dragons were created to protect the world, and were meant to bring balance between the humans and elementals. Many years ago that changed and the current Dragons allowed their purpose to be corrupted. Now their time is at an end. The next Black Dragon has been born, and in twenty years she will visit this temple with her mates." His fanged mouth dipped low. "And you will be ready for them."

"But the Dragons have ruled for as long as anyone can remember," Derel said. "How can they be replaced?"

"The Dragons were only meant to rule for a short time, before passing the torch to the next generation. Nysa and her mates defied the Gods to gain immortality. Now their rule must come to an end."

I glanced at my mates again, the four men I loved, and

knew they'd stand beside me no matter what we faced. If our purpose was to prepare for these ascendants, we'd be ready. If we had to defy the Dragons, we'd do it.

I stepped forward and gazed up at the fiery god. "We're ready to serve."

CHAPTER FIFTEEN

TWENTY YEARS LATER

I stood in front of the temple and gazed out across the barren landscape surrounding the volcano. Small figures approached in the distance on horseback, getting closer with every minute. Purpose and determination smoldered inside me, along with the Fire God's flames. I'd waited for this day for twenty years and it was hard to believe this moment was finally here.

I turned around and headed back through the temple, where my four mates waited for me. Blane, Roth, Derel, and Falon all wore the red and black robes of the Fire God's priests and I gazed at each of them with love nearly bursting inside of me. Even after twenty years together, we were still as much in love as when we first came to the temple, if not more so. Every day we'd spent together was a true blessing, and I was so thankful the Fire God chose me—and that these four men had agreed to become my priests.

"It's time," I said.

"The new Black Dragon?" Blane asked, arching an eyebrow.

I nodded. "She and her mates are approaching now. They should be here in a few hours."

"I'll start preparing a feast," Derel said. "They're going to be hungry after they climb that mountain."

"I'll prepare the bonding room," Falon said, glancing back at the room with the altar and the bed that we rarely went into, which had been waiting for the ascendants all this time.

"Thank you," I told them both with a smile.

"Any sign of the other Dragons?" Roth asked. "Sark?"

"Not yet." I glanced back at the smoke-filled sky. The Fire God had kept his promise and the volcano had been quiet for the entire time we'd lived here—until now. We all knew what that meant, and were prepared to leave on a moment's notice if needed. "But I'm glad we sent the children to Sparkport, just in case."

I'd been blessed with four children, one from each of my mates, which we considered gifts from the Fire God. Our oldest daughter would one day become the High Priestess after me, if she wished to take that role. For now, they were safe at the bakery with Loka and her wife. Once this was over, we'd be reunited again.

Though the Fire God had never appeared to me again, I knew he'd been watching over us, waiting for this day. He'd given me purpose, and over the years I'd devoured every book in the library and studied up on the Dragons, or what little was left about them anyway, while my mates and I prepared as best we could for the new Dragons' arrival. Change was coming to the four Realms, but if our plans were successful, we would no longer live under Nysa's oppressive regime. Soon the new Black Dragon would rise, with her four mates at her side. Only then would balance return to the world.

While the men took care of final preparations, I dressed in my ceremonial robes and waited for the ascendants to climb the volcano, much like we'd done years ago. Until, hours later, a young woman with red hair took the final steps onto the summit of Valefire, with her mates at her side.

It was time to meet the people who would save the world.

Ready to find out how Calla and her mates help the ascendants defeat the Dragons?

Turn the page to read the first chapter from the next book in the series about Kira and her mates, *Stroke The Flame...*

CHAPTER ONE

KIRA

I crept through the forest in search of my prey, my hand tight on my bow. Heavy rain left a sheen of water on my face even with my hood covering me, and I wiped it off on my already-soaked sleeve. The storm was getting stronger. If I didn't find a deer or something else soon, I'd have to give up and return empty-handed. Roark wouldn't like that.

I made my way toward one of my traps up ahead, stepping carefully through the high brush and keeping my eyes peeled for any game. With the weather as it was, I doubted I would have any luck. All the animals in the forest had no doubt retreated once this sudden storm had come upon us. The only thing left out here would be elementals and shades—and I had no desire to confront either of those.

When I'd set out a few hours ago, the sky had been clear and bright. Only in the last hour had the storm clouds gathered overhead as if out of nowhere, or perhaps summoned by the Gods themselves. I shivered, and not just from the cold that sank into my bones through my soaked clothes.

I bent down to check the trap I'd left this morning and breathed a sigh of relief. A large rabbit had been caught inside. Tonight I'd be fed. Tonight Tash would be safe.

I tossed the rabbit into a sack and loaded it onto my shoulder. When I turned around, I wasn't alone. I dropped the sack and aimed my bow, my heart in my throat.

An old woman stood before me, her body hunched over with age, her skin pale and wrinkled. She wore a frayed traveling cloak and frizzy white hair escaped her low hood. I might have heard her as she approached, but the storm drowned out all sound except for the pounding of rain in the trees.

"Can I help you?" I called out to her, as I lowered my bow and retrieved my fallen sack.

"Perhaps." She stared at me and frowned, then looked around as if confused.

"You must be lost. I can show you to Stoneham, the nearest town."

"That's kind of you."

I offered her my arm and she took it, leaning upon me. Her grip was strong, even though she seemed so frail I worried a strong gust might turn her bones to dust. I wondered how she had found herself in the middle of the forest in the first place. She shouldn't be traveling alone, especially not in this weather.

"What's your name?" she asked.

"Kira."

As we carefully stepped through the forest she gazed up at the dark sky, letting the rain wash over her face. "There's a storm coming."

I patted her wrinkled hand where it rested on my arm. "I think it's already here. But if we hurry, we can get out of it. The inn is just ahead."

"There's no escaping this storm." She turned toward me and her eyes were like steel. "Not for you."

Her words sent another shiver down my spine. "I'm not sure what you mean."

She held my gaze another few seconds, then waved her hand. "Just the ramblings of an old woman. Nothing more."

I frowned, but continued walking through the wet brush. "We're nearly there now."

"Yes, indeed we are," she said.

A rustling sound up ahead caught my attention. I dropped her arm and drew my bow. "Stay back. I'll make sure the way is clear."

I took a step forward as I peered through the brush in front of us, watching for the slightest twitch of a leaf or the dash of fur. But there was nothing other than the relentless rain.

When I turned back, the woman was gone.

"Hello?" I called out, spinning around and scanning the area for her. The storm made it hard to see anything, but there was no trace of her anywhere. She'd just...vanished.

I went back the way we'd walked, calling out for the woman, but I couldn't find her anywhere. There was no sign she'd ever been in the forest at all.

After many long minutes, with the rain pounding down on me and the wind whipping at my cloak, I reluctantly gave up my search. I told myself she must have gone ahead to the village without me, but something about that didn't feel right. It was the only explanation though, unless she was a shade. But if that were true I wouldn't still be breathing, according to the stories I'd heard anyway. I'd never actually seen a shade before, but it was said they were ghostly figures that could turn invisible, pass through walls, and suck the life right out of you. As strange as the woman was, she seemed perfectly human at least. Still, probably best for me to hurry back.

I headed toward the inn, more by instinct than sight at this point. As I left the forest, my shoes sank into the mud and the relentless wind tore the hood off my head. I tried to tug it back on, but there was no use. My hair was already soaked through and I was chilled to the bone.

Lightning flashed overhead, followed immediately by the deep rumble of thunder. I ran for the inn as fast as I could, but the wind was so strong it seemed to push me back, as if it was fighting my every step. I slipped in the mud and fell to my knees, bracing myself with my hands. The impact jolted through my bones, and for a moment I could only remain there, dazed and covered in mud from head to toe.

As I tried to stand, a bright crack lit up the sky, blinding me. Searing hot pain struck my head and I screamed as a bolt of lightning coursed through me. Electricity spread within my entire body, setting every nerve on fire and burning me from the inside out. It raced through my blood, and I thought my heart would burst from the power warring for control within me. Time stopped, and pain became the only thing I knew.

And then it was gone.

Deep, cavernous thunder sounded all around me as my sight returned. My entire body shook and trembled uncontrollably. Mud covered me completely, rain pelted my face, wind lashed at my hair, and sparks danced in my blood. As if the elemental Gods themselves had thought to strike me down, then decided to let me live after all.

I scrambled back to my feet, nearly slipping again in the slick mud. When I was steady, I grabbed the bag with the rabbit from where I'd dropped it, before stumbling to the back door of the inn. I opened the door with some effort, the wind battling me still, and then stepped inside the familiar warm kitchen that smelled of stew and baked bread. Once the door was shut, I fell back against it, breathing heavily.

I'd been struck by lightning. Yet somehow I still lived.

I quickly checked my body, searching for signs of injury, but I seemed to be physically fine, although my cloak was charred and I was in great need of a bath. The only thing that afflicted me was shock.

None of it made sense. Lightning usually hit the tallest thing around, and I was nowhere near that. I'd been surrounded by much better targets. The inn. The stables. The trees. Why had it hit me?

And how had I made it through without a scratch?

ABOUT THE AUTHOR

New York Times Bestselling Author Elizabeth Briggs writes unputdownable romance across genres with bold heroines and fearless heroes. She graduated from UCLA with a degree in Sociology and has worked for an international law firm, mentored teens in writing, and volunteered with dog rescue groups. Now she's a full-time geek who lives in Los Angeles with her husband and a pack of fluffy dogs.

Visit Elizabeth's website: www.elizabethbriggs.net

ALSO BY ELIZABETH BRIGGS

Her Elemental Dragons

Light the Fire

Stroke The Flame

Kiss The Sky

Shake The Earth

Ride The Wave

The Chasing The Dream Series

More Than Exes

More Than Music

More Than Comics

More Than Fashion

More Than Once

More Than Distance

The Future Shock Trilogy

Future Shock

Future Threat

Future Lost

Hollywood Roommates

Made in the USA
Columbia, SC
02 September 2021

44764968R00069